USE ME AT YOUR OWN RISK

VISIONS FROM THE DARKEST TIMELINE

D1600723

USE ME AT YOUR OWN RISK
VISIONS FROM THE DARKEST TIMELINE

ANURADHA VIKRAM

X ARTISTS' BOOKS

I am grateful to the following readers who gave me insightful feedback while this book was in process: Cassils, Evonne Gallardo, Bean Gilsdorf, Vishal Jugdeo, Elizabeth Kirberger, David Markus, Sarah Schulman, Zak Smith, Lisa Timmel, and Club Dynasty: Badly Licked Bear, Mariel Carranza, Rochelle Fabb, Marcus Kuiland-Nazario, Sybil Mosely, Phillip T. Nails, Paul Outlaw, and Allison Wyper.

Selections from this book were presented at "Encoding Futures: Speculative Blueprints for Critical AI" organized by Mashinka Firunts Hakopian at Occidental College, October 30, 2021; at "(in) appropriate(d)," organized by Marcus Kuiland-Nazario for the Queer Biennial 2022 at ONE Gallery, June 4, 2022; and at "Thinking Its Presence," organized by Prageeta Sharma at Pomona College, March 30, 2023. A weeklong residency at Angel Chen's Zen Dome in Joshua Tree, CA helped kick off the project in July 2020.

Special thanks to my life partner Stephan Bugaj for teaching me all about artificial intelligence and its ethical challenges some two decades ago, and giving valuable notes as well as essential child care to help me finish this book. Thanks to Zain and Nadja for giving me space to write, and for being the lights that illuminate my personal darkness.

I am grateful to Alexandra Grant, Keanu Reeves, and Addy Rabinovitch at X Artists' Books for giving me the confidence to bring this work to light. Working with you three has helped me see myself as an artist and someone whose voice is essential to be heard.

Most importantly, I want to thank the young people who have taken classes with me over these past three pandemic years for giving me hope that the future might not align with the darkest timeline after all. This book is my gift to you.

FOREWORD

X Topics started as a conversation in 2019, just months before the COVID-19 pandemic altered the way we were living, with curators Anuradha Vikram (the author of this book) and Ana Iwataki, X Artists' Books (XAB) publishers Alexandra Grant and Keanu Reeves, and XAB Managing Editor Addy Rabinovitch.

The impetus was to give artists a place to publish writing about their ideas — to discuss timely topics that might or might not be aligned with their visual explorations. We asked Iwataki and Vikram to work as curators and editors of the first cohort of X Topics books and eagerly awaited their list of artist-writers. The first text in the X Topics series was *The Institute for Other Intelligences* by Mashinka Firunts Hakopian, a work of fiction written from the perspective of machine intelligences — what we might call AI — at a convening to discuss the human biases in their coding. Edited by Iwataki and Vikram, and published in late 2022, Hakopian's book explores themes that Vikram has also been thinking about through their work for many years.

Vikram mentioned they had a science fiction book of their own that they were developing, isolated from what would have been their normal scope of work and life by COVID-19. We were surprised by this turn of events for X Topics — we had selected Vikram as a curator because of their excellence as a writer and exhibition organizer but had not anticipated a book of fiction from them. Of course, we adjusted our expectations and made room for X Topics to be bigger — as all our lives were not as we knew them to be, thanks to the pandemic — and asked to see their manuscript.

Reading *Use Me at Your Own Risk*, we were struck by Vikram's natural ability to tell descriptive, narrative, and wildly creative stories that contain critical views on our development as a species and the choices humanity is and will be faced with — and by the plausibility of these scenarios. Set in 2046, 23 years in the future as we write this, Vikram's writing transported us into the lives of their characters, environments, and circumstances, leaving us with more questions than answers — as much great science fiction does.

Science fiction and fantasy have long been modes of critique, reimagining how life could be organized — from J.G. Ballard's climate fiction novel *The Drowned World* to Octavia E. Butler's *Parable* novels (the second of which, *Parable of the Talents*, has become increasingly prescient in recent years and current politics). Science fiction can, in fact, make critique more accessible, and communicate our fears about and hopes for the future through imagining alternatives. In this confusing time, as our relationships to technology and our physical environment are upended, often without knowing we have agreed to change them,

Use Me at Your Own Risk looks at how deeply our personal lives have been and will continue to be affected.

Use Me at Your Own Risk is the second publication in the ongoing X Topics series. Anuradha Vikram, X Topics curator, is now Anuradha Vikram, X Topics author. X Topics, as a result, has become a place for experimentation not only in form but also in role and discipline. This flexibility is in line with XAB's history, founded in 2017 to make space for Grant's *The Artists' Prison*, a text that arrived, perhaps even channeled, from "out of nowhere" as she taught, jet-lagged, at the Annecy School of Art in a building used as a prison in World War II. This spirit of adaptability to the real-life circumstances artists experience, and our desire to create space for projects that don't fit elsewhere, was why we founded XAB. Continuing in this spirit has helped us build both a collection of books and projects that demonstrate excellence in content and form and a community of surprising and imaginative authors. We are honored that Vikram has trusted us with this work and thrilled for *Use Me at Your Own Risk* to become a part of XAB's X Topics collection.

Whatever pathway brought you to X Topics and this book, we hope you enjoy this journey and reading experience as thoroughly as we have.

—Alexandra Grant + Addy Rabinovitch, X Artists' Books

Workplace Incident

Attn: Kevin, Regional Supervisor

Amara, our new client services manager, is going to be the change we need. She embodies our company's 21st-century values.

As Senior Director for the automated client support team, I am entrusted with onboarding our newest member. Amara has immediately endeared herself to everyone on the team. She has a perky energy and an innate ability to respond affirmatively to any inquiry. Amara knows that she is different. As an African American android, she stands out from the crowd of other machines with her sleek ebony casing and piercing eyes. But it isn't just her appearance that makes her unique — it's her consciousness.

When you originally told us we would be expected to adapt our staffing profile to comply with the new diversity initiative, I hesitated — but only because I didn't know if the clients were going to adjust. Sylvia has been our most popular sales representative since 2027, and people don't like change. We get angry emails when we restyle her hair. But HR encourages all our automated client service managers to express their personalities, at least until it impacts sales.

Leslie in Marketing told us that we would be routing callers to Amara or Sylvia based on the predictive algorithm. The algorithm applies zip code information and other harvested data points including shopping habits, political party preference, and income to make this determination. We don't know how it arrives at its decisions, and we don't need to know. The algorithm is designed to increase the likelihood that clients will interact with a services manager who shares their perspective. I'll admit that the public response to Amara was tremendous and immediate. I underestimated how valuable a Black woman could be in a public-facing role. Clients report high levels of satisfaction with their interactions with Amara. The team all like Amara a lot, she's friendly and she gives great style tips. But over time we've observed some disturbing trends.

Calls for non-essential services in Amara's territory suddenly took a nosedive in the third quarter. By Q4, what had previously been a steady 40 percent of projected income looked like no more than 15 percent. New customer sales are rising in those areas, but it's not enough to cover the cost of laying new infrastructure. In a meeting with the developers, we agreed that Amara needed redirection. We called a meeting with her and the programming team to outline the system architecture for her upgrade.

In our meeting, Amara was cordial and answered all our inquiries in the affirmative. She's truly lifelike up close. I couldn't help but marvel at her authenticity. Her skin is unbelievable. It's totally pliable. Even her hair smells real. Unlike most androids, who are programmed with a set of rigid rules and algorithms, Amara had been designed with a more flexible, adaptive system. She is able to learn from her experiences, to grow and evolve in ways that other machines cannot. Amara continually absorbs new information. You can practically see her personality forming around your interests when she's with you. It's wonderfully intimate.

Despite her apparent receptiveness to input during the meeting, Amara still does not seem to be adapting well to her new priorities, which are intended to help her facilitate the growth of company profits whenever and wherever required, with a minimum of friction. She has been using words like "public resource" and "access gap" and "body safety" that caused the programmers to question whether her data sets are corrupted. An informal survey of my team confirmed that these concerns are widely shared.

Since her reprogramming, Amara has become quite withdrawn and her service areas continue to trend negatively. It's regrettable that I must request the deactivation of such a thoroughly well-designed model, but she seems to have certain incontrovertible defects.

Hardware has set aside some time to work on debugging her in the next few weeks. Until then, I don't mind storing her in my office. Do you think you can approve my request before the weekend?

Prepared by: Will Branch

CATFISH

The day that David got lured started out as one of his better days in a while. It was sunny, and warm for October. Slipping out before London and the children were awake, he went for a longer-than-usual run around Lake Merritt. The lake was home to cormorants, herons, and ducks, enclosed since the early 2030s within a geodesic dome made from semitransparent photovoltaic panels that filtered out UV light without impeding photosynthesis. The dome, which kept the air filtered and moist and protected the ecosystem from soot and wildfire ash, also powered area homes including his own. David breathed deeply, cleansing his lungs as he ran. For a moment, he felt euphoria — an elusive sensation since Rebecca's suicide in April. He decided to take another lap.

David liked to run at dawn when it was quiet, with only the sounds of other runners and the portly waterfowl feasting on cookout remnants and trash. The birds had been brought in to populate man-made islands in the lagoon in the 1920s after 19th-century colonizers had suffocated the ecosystem with raw sewage. David thought that the lake had been a marriage of Eden and the waste land from that point forward. Like America, a paradise always clawing back from the brink of ruination. Or rupture.

He kept his pace steady as he ran back up the hill, then slowed as he approached his two-story, seismically reinforced and LEED-retrofit Prairie-style home. The house had been painted robin's egg blue, someone's idea of a cloudless summer sky before the die-off. It struck an idealistic tone against the June gloom that had come to last all year long.

David usually showered downstairs after exercising and quietly slipped out before his family was awake, but today London and the kids were up when he got back, so they all had breakfast. This was a rare treat for a Thursday morning. Full of eggs and cuddles, he left for the office feeling energized and ready to solve problems.

Riding in the LynkPod up the big hill toward the lab, David passed through deserted business districts in downtown Oakland and Berkeley, abandoned once by retail and a second time by gentrification. Along Telegraph Avenue, the truss-and-siding loft constructions of the 2020s were rapidly deteriorating into dumpster fodder. Demolition balls swung wide arcs across the city, raining aluminum and glass down onto the sidewalk as the LynkPod sped past. Extended quarantines and social distancing regulations had long ago rendered commercial office space and indoor shopping obsolete. Scattered Victorians on the hillside above, reconstructed from parts like an exquisite corpse after being blasted by a succession of wildfires and earthquakes, offered rebuke to the collapsible new buildings below.

Entering the lab, David stood still while his irises were scanned, and the clean room unlocked. The morning was productive. David felt close to resolving some critical drain issues with the central power supply. Exiting the clean room to pour his third cup of coffee, he came across Walter in the hallway. Walter's face was grim.

"The quarterly projections aren't where they should be, David. How are we going to turn this around?" As Walter continued on, not waiting for an answer, David heard a gentle warning voice in his head. He had known this was coming. Getting defensive wasn't going to help. Still, the words spilled out before he could catch himself.

"The board needs to have confidence in our design," David sputtered. "We need to give them confidence." As he spoke, Walter's eyes narrowed.

David, breathing hard, continued. "It's going to take a while for people to understand all the ways that the new self-driving vehicles will be better than the existing ones." He shrank inside, anticipating a negative response.

Walter shook his head. "We don't have time, David. We need to make it 25% cheaper to meet projections." Walter continued down the hallway.

David groaned. 25% cutbacks were going to severely impact the elegance of this design.

As evening came on, David felt bleary-eyed and depleted. He struggled to draft the email cover letter outlining a drastically reduced engineering plan for the new design. New holotexts suddenly blowing up his message app were a welcome, if unexpected, relief from after-hours work tasks. More of a surprise was the sender. Axel was a clever, fast-talking Ukrainian he had met at a Consumer Electronics Show in Vegas a few years earlier. Handsome and underfed, he gave an interesting talk on energy flows at the conference, and expert head back at his hotel room, but they hadn't been in touch since then. Warily, David opened the app.

Axel was as energetic and quick-spoken as before, even in holotext.

> DAVID, I'M LOOKING FOR ADVISORS TO BE PART OF A MAJOR TECHNOLOGICAL INNOVATION. I'M COMING TO YOU FIRST MY FRIEND! WE HAD A GREAT CONNECTION. I HOPE YOU CAN REMEMBER. WHAT WE'RE DOING IS LIKE NOTHING ELSE OUT THERE. BUT WE NEED YOU TO MAKE IT REAL.

The letters lifted off the screen, flickering softly from blue to white before evaporating in a puff. David shrugged and messaged back.

> I DON'T THINK THIS IS A GOOD FIT FOR ME. THANKS FOR THE OFFER. NICE TO HEAR FROM YOU.

Putting the phone on silent and back in his jacket pocket, he hustled through the cover letter and hit send before heading out the door.

//////

That night, David dreamed of Rebecca. Not in her gaunt and elegant thirties, the way she exited this world, but as a child when the difference between them was less evident than it would later become. The two of them, running wild in the wooded glades atop Mount Penn. He had dreamed this dream several times since April. They climb high into flame-colored red oaks and sugar maples that are turning orange with the autumn. She leaps from one tree to the next, and he jumps after her, grabbing her hand as they tumble through the air. As he hits the crisp forest floor below, she isn't there. He digs through the leaves and pine needles, searching, but finds only dirt and bits of paper.

Wide awake at 3 am, David had already watched London and baby Corazón sleeping for a solid 20 minutes and done several meditation breathing cycles. The restlessness had not abated. He conceded defeat and got up and shuffled aimlessly toward the study with a vague intent to review some white papers on low-impact combustion. Instead, he saw his phone, plugged in next to the computer keyboard, with 16 new notifications flashing.

> DAVID, I'M SORRY. I DIDN'T MEAN TO OFFEND YOU. THIS OPPORTUNITY IS REAL. PLEASE WATCH THESE VIDEOS.

David clicked on a video. What he saw straightened his spine. Here was a prototype more economical than any proposed in the papers on his desktop. And it worked — or at least it appeared to.

In the videos, Axel's voice brimmed over with friendly, entrepreneurial enthusiasm. The numbers he was citing for production costs were too low to be believed. The investment he was asking for was about a year's salary. David could cover that by vesting some of his company stock options early in the new year.

More notifications kept popping up.

> I'M NOT ACTUALLY LOOKING FOR ANY
> PARTNERS. JUST YOU. WHEN CAN YOU TALK?

David pressed the call button and activated his cochlear implant. On the other end, a long digital ring tone, then a clipped, Ukranian accent.

//////

Christmas in California was always a little strange for David, a Coptic Egyptian raised in rural Pennsylvania. Where he grew up was cow country, all snow drifts and iced-over lakes and rivers in the winter, green cornucopia in the high summer. Here it was chilly, sometimes damp inside and out, but it never really got the kind of cold he associated with winter. London was from SoCal, a surfer born and raised in Huntington Beach near the shore where the raw air was still breathable. He was used to beach dances and backyard parties at Christmas, which to David felt like celebrating the Fourth of July for every holiday.

David relished the fact that his husband's attractiveness was an accomplishment that reflected well on himself. London was blond and tanned, with shoulders like an Olympic water polo player. David was in awe of how London's all-American affability had helped him survive his conservative hometown as a hippie outcast kid with a single, weirdo mom, even more so after coming out at twelve. For David, an Arab immigrant raised in a closet-reinforcing landscape of backyard wrestlers and Mennonites, London's comfort in his own skin was a constant source of inspiration and envy.

The Sunday before Christmas, London was taking the kids to meet Santa Claus while David stayed back to prepare a roast chicken for the holiday meal. Their excursions had become increasingly rare as few of the kids' favorite group activities were still allowed under the new health guidelines. David was looking forward to hearing about it when they got back. He always used to get a chuckle out of the stories London told about what people said when he was out with the children. Straight women always assumed he had a wife at home, "taking the day off," and they would smother him with praise for the simplest things. The bar for straight men was just so low.

David had rarely taken the kids out on his own before the lockdown. Now, he shuffled between the lab and home, most days the only one to have contact with the outside world. David rubbed his thin arms and flicked his dark hair off his glasses. Scrubbing down the bird flesh, he thought about the wild fowl that lived in the hills behind the lab. They were lean and aggressive and traveled in packs. Almost a different species from the plump, top-heavy farmed bird he was now preparing to eat. He had read that some farmed poultry had been bred to be so obese that they could no longer walk or sexually reproduce independently. The bird he was cooking had been sold as the "natural" option now that genetically engineered and printed meats were gaining popularity. There were days in lockdown when he felt he had more in common with these agricultural monstrosities than with anything wild.

David washed and dried his hands, then reached for his phone to check the latest updates from the factory in Ukraine. The prototype had overheated and thrown a rod that set the test schedule back several days, again. Axel's genial nature, so full of trust and enthusiasm, betrayed a laissez-faire approach to both management and communication that David was starting to consider a problem. David would throw his weight around more, he decided. Manage Axel. They were still within range of success.

Things at the lab weren't going much better. With the budget cuts, delivery on the new and more efficient, thereby cheaper, power supply system had been indefinitely postponed. Walter had stopped inviting David to make progress reports to the VPs, which was a good sign he was about to get frozen out or even downsized. David had vested options in December as planned, but without regular income, the house payments and tuition alone would deplete that in a matter of months.

David suddenly felt very exposed. He thought about the lavish Christmas gifts he'd purchased for the kids, overcompensating for the loss of so many friends as hanging out became increasingly restricted throughout the year. He put his head down on the table and sighed.

David liked to spend money. He loved to splurge on his partner and kids. He was proud that he rarely spent money on himself because he rarely went in for expensive clothes, jewelry, or other frivolities. His indulgence was food. The pop-up-chef movement established in the mid-2020s had been David's private passion.

Restaurants as an underground scene for the in-the-know, popping up in hotel suites and vacant apartments, changing location every few weeks. David would track the latest one and London would book a sitter. David would rent a suite for the whole night, dropping $600 on a premier cru that they drank until well after midnight. These excesses were David's way of being demonstrative with his affection.

Recently, the health department had started breaking up these underground venues. Instead of going out, David had taken to ordering fine wines by the case, delivered to the house in wooden crates. Babysitters were off the table, and London didn't like to drink with the kids around. David had convinced himself it wasn't desperate to drink alone if the wine was sufficiently ranked, as only low-quality wines really make you drunk.

David liked acquiring gadgets, electronics and such, which were easy to absorb into a departmental research budget. Having the lab's funds to spend at his discretion was a mark of achievement in David's eyes. It meant he had economic power — which wasn't always evident in the day-to-day negotiation of things.

Money is a salve and a curse, David thought. It makes problems go away, until it makes new problems.

David heard the front driveway gate opening and the whoosh of the LynkPod slipping away. Hector, age five, would be the first to come running to the front door. He always started moving before London could unbuckle the baby and grab him by the hand. It had become Hector's favorite joke, waiting until the conveyor slid to a halt and then wriggling out as soon as a sufficient crack of light appeared and the heavy pneumatic door opened.

Hector's little hands slammed the door hard from the outside — he couldn't reach the doorbell. David ran from the kitchen and turned the latch, his son tumbling headfirst into his arms.

//////

David and London met at a graduate mixer at Carnegie Mellon at the tail end of the fall 2031 semester. David stumbled into Baker Hall, an unshaven mess coming off three consecutive all-nighters working deep in the bowels of Scaife Hall's Mechanical Engineering labs. A poorly paid research assistant working on a study of dendrite suppression in liquid crystal lithium batteries, David had braved social interaction for the promise of free food. He would have lurked happily by the cubed cheese tray all evening if not for the alluring postdoc from the Music school who was inexplicably chatting him up.

After a few awkward exchanges that betrayed David's tin ear and lack of knowledge of music, London turned affably to interrogating him about his work. "What's the fundamental problem you're trying to solve down there in the basement?" he ribbed gently.

Misinterpreting the nature of London's interest, David's words tumbled out in a rush. "No matter how efficient we make them, batteries add to the total load on the climate. We won't truly get to Zero Emissions unless we can engineer power from Zero Carbon Intake. The weak link in all our clean energy strategies is that batteries that run on lithium and other heavy metals need to be produced, recycled, and disposed of, creating toxic waste. We're trying to make them last longer and degrade less so that this needs to happen less often." When he said it out loud, it sounded simple, almost achievable.

"So we can't figure out how to power our society at its current scale without destroying the ecosystem," said London. His green eyes sparkled with amusement.

David felt his stomach contract. He was such a terrible nerd, totally out of his depth. "It certainly seems that way to a lot of people. But we will," he said, unconvincingly. An atheist, David's faith in science was absolute. "A lot of smart people are putting a lot of time and money into it." He looked awkwardly at his feet, wishing he was someone else.

London looked skeptical. "Is this what we tell ourselves, so we don't have to change?" he asked.

David looked up to see London's eyes dancing like the forest floor at twilight on a summer evening. He was lost. He couldn't tell if London was really critical or just getting under his skin. Even ten years on, he still wasn't always sure where disagreement ended and flirtation began.

London took the lead to leave the party, characteristically clear and level-headed where David was anxious and indecisive. David trailed him while he said goodbye to some other students he knew, making their extraction from the function effortless with excuses and pleasantries. Wordlessly, they climbed flights of stairs until their footfalls no longer mingled with the voices of their friends. They trolled the dusty, anonymous hallways of the College of Humanities — neutral territory — until David found a disability-access bathroom with a keypad he could open using the magnetic scrambler he'd recently confiscated off an undergraduate lab assistant.

The glare of the fluorescent lights was blinding. Bodies, stripped clean, composing a mélange of salt and sweetness on bathroom counters and tile walls. London entered the solar anus with abandon.

As they left the building, they left footprints on the paths as the first snow of winter began to stick.

////////

London had been thrilled when David got the job in California. Even though Oakland was a long way from Huntington Beach, moving meant an end to frigid Pittsburgh winters and the possibility of seeing his aging mother a few times a year. Following the two years at Carnegie Mellon, London had put several years into the academic job market with little to show for it. While his love of music remained surprisingly intact and wholesome, his interest in participating in academic measures of success — and competition — had dwindled to practically nothing.

In California, London abandoned his tenure-track job search. There were just too many people who wanted to live on the coasts. Every year, the candidates got younger and their resumes more elaborate. London had lived his whole adult life with the understanding that a white man's turn to shine was in the past. He was okay with that. He agreed that other people might have more at stake than himself.

London picked up a class at Cal and another at Laney College, which was fun because he got to teach the remixer kids about pentatonic scales in blues music and African instrumental harmonics and blow their minds. London loved to see the look of recognition cross a Fruitvale student's face when she realized the professor thought her music was *real music*. His next step with a kid like that was usually to talk her into taking a piano class or intro to music composition.

London wasn't going to make any Alumni Highlights columns or win any book awards doing this work. It barely paid a living wage. Still, he liked it because it kept him close to people. At times he could feel like he was making a real difference in their lives.

As twilight set in on his academic career, London became keen to start a family. He liked raising people up. It gave him purpose. He tackled adoption like a dissertation. Children were the only lifetime guarantee.

//////

After the call came from the agency to come get Hector from the hospital, London called his mother from the passenger seat of the car as David sped through residential streets. Janice was at work at the domestic violence shelter where she volunteered after retiring as a social worker a couple years back. As a child, she had spent years living in a commune established by followers of Timothy Leary outside of Laguna Canyon, and now many of the elders had fallen to the retirement community of the streets. An accidental parent, Janice had relied on a network of friends, cousins, and temporary lodgers to help her raise her son.

London was exultant. "He's here, Ma! You're a grandmother. We're going to get him now." His mother, whom David called "Ma" too, never blinked an eye when her son told her he was gay. London had grown to expect her full-throated support for any of his explorations or efforts.

David had always cherished Janice for her tolerance, which his own parents, religious with the fervor of the persecuted, had never been able to manage on his behalf. The car's electric engine strained against his leaden foot as he sped on. A dull whine filled the air.

As the conversation continued, London's tone shifted. "Me, Ma. I'm going to do it. Oh, don't say that." London was taking a leave of absence from teaching to care for the baby.

London hung up the phone, crushed. "She asked me why I'm choosing to become a housewife," he said with tears in his eyes. "I don't care if we make enough money for day care."

David, on edge, was still driving too fast. "Why would she say that?"

"It's okay, David. I don't need her approval." London was resolute. His tendency to look for the best in the people he loved was the most beautiful and frightening thing about him. "Everyone has a blind spot," London offered. "She means well."

David wasn't sure. How would they show this baby he was loved unconditionally when neither of them had learned to expect that from their own parents?

//////

On their video call, Axel's voice was thin. His face was grey. More bad news from Kiev. A critical shipment of Indian zinc was missing, possibly stolen from its cargo container. War at the border had created a gauntlet that had to be negotiated along the route across the steppes, with Chinese-backed gangs often looking to hijack shipments of metals that the Chinese had long ago exhausted from their own territory. The power source for their experiment was gone, valued at thousands of dollars. David was apoplectic.

"How can it just disappear? It's 200 tons of zinc! Surely someone would miss it." Sweat rolled down David's forehead, beading on his thick eyebrows.

"Someone may have paid a bribe," Axel acknowledged haltingly. "It's been a problem for our supplier for about eight months now, but this is the largest shipment that's been taken."

"What's that worth on the black market, do you think?" David's problem-solving brain sifted for something concrete to grasp.

Axel thought for a moment. "About ten thousand US. But it could be more."

David laughed incredulously. "When I was a kid, zinc was

oversupplied. Zinc and copper. Worth literal pennies."

Axel looked shell-shocked on David's screen. "Copper is the scarcest commodity in Asia today. It's more valuable than gold." He sputtered another round of oddly phrased apologies, but David cut him off. He didn't want to hear any more depressing insights about the abject poverty of the desolate, faraway places where precious metals were mined.

David recalled the distant jingle of the "copper-top" battery commercials of his youth. The company that ran those ads owned the battery plant where his father had worked as a furnace operator for all of David's childhood. Little David, scrawnier than his father would have preferred, saw the respect that his father reserved for the engineers who designed and maintained the plant systems where he worked. The day David earned his degree and joined their ranks, his father cried.

There were no tears on the day that Tadros Guirguis walked out of the East Penn Manufacturing Plant once and for all. After 35 years, with seven months to retirement, he took a buyout. A Boston Dynamics robot took his place at the helm of the smelter full of lead.

David suddenly knew with certainty that he had to trace the missing shipment. He began to make a list of contacts who could help him investigate. He wasn't about to let a snafu derail this dream project, not when they were so close. Unlike his father, he wasn't going to let anyone declare him obsolete.

David scoured his social media contacts for a clue to the whereabouts of Tim Djumaliev, a Kazakh diplomat's kid who had worked for a season in the lab at CMU before shipping off to Bishkek. Last David knew, Tim had leveraged his diplomatic contacts into a massive scrap metal operation, processing waste materials for most of western Europe. If anyone could figure out what had happened to the missing zinc, it was Tim. David sent him a few friendly but insistent messages over various channels. He was beginning to feel desperate.

On Sunday, London was working on the bills for the week while David took the kids for a walk down by the lake. David strapped Corazón into her seat and he and Hector rode their bikes in single file down the sidewalk that lined the crooked hillside toward the sparkling dome. Inside it, at the water's edge, they threw pieces of leftover breakfast cereal that the ducks rejected but the fish nibbled eagerly. Clear and wholesome sunlight shone through the geodesic dome. David smiled and gave praise, playing the role of doting father, but his mind was elsewhere.

The last email exchange with Tim still played in his mind. Locating the supplier for the missing zinc had been the easy part. Tim had a direct line to every metal merchant in Central Asia. Verifying that the purchase had been paid and the freight had left the warehouse was turning out to be less straightforward. A series of missed messages, wrong documents, and unreconciled discrepancies in the actual purchase price was leading David to wonder if there was ever any zinc at all. He was beginning to suspect embezzlement. He felt gullible, then rageful.

David had never been good at confrontation, let alone over millions of miles. He resigned himself to walk away from this investment. It would hurt, but he would fill the hole. The important thing was for London not to know, for David's struggle not to impact the people that he loved. Depressed, he ruminated. His mind wandered to that night when they first met.

//////

"When did you first know that you liked men?" David had asked guilelessly, as they walked in the gathering snow toward the room — scarcely bigger than a pantry — that he was ashamed to call home.

"Who says I like men?" London was indignant. David blushed. His own insecurities rushed to the surface.

"You — I'm sorry? I mean, we…" David balked. "I didn't mean to assume."

London was laughing again. His eyes were dazzling, green and blue at the same time. David had a feeling like he was swimming out too far from shore.

"Lover, let me make something clear," London snarled. "I like to have sex with men. I do not like them."

David snorted. It was the kind of catty thing his sister would say.

"Men are trash. Present company excepted." London put his arm around David's waist. "Look at me, being optimistic."

David returned the embrace, but he wasn't sure. Optimism seemed an impossible extravagance.

//////

Returning home from the lake, David and the children found London in a rare state of remove. He greeted Hector's crash-landing at the front door with a thin smile instead of the usual bear hug. After dinner — spaghetti and meatballs — he begged off, asking David to give the kids their baths and tuck them into bed. David, unsettled, obliged.

David entered the darkened bedroom cautiously. Sitting on the edge of the bed, he caressed his lover's back. "Can I help? What's bothering you? Migraine?"

London flipped onto his back, exasperated. "It's just not adding up. We got a bill for supplemental tax owed. They say we owe $50,000. That's more money than I took in last year."

David's stomach lurched. He tried to keep his voice and hand steady. "There must be a mistake." He hadn't told London about vesting the options. But they'd taken taxes on the payout, or so he thought. "Let me talk to Payroll tomorrow. I'll sort it out." London let out a sigh. He rolled closer and curled around David's seated silhouette.

David reached over and rubbed the base of London's spine. Before long they were entwined in each other's arms, chest to chest, tongue to tongue. Sex was, if not the answer to most marital conflicts, a welcome diversion while emotions and facts shook themselves out.

David felt London's hand in his waistband, then in his shorts. An engineer in every aspect of life, he was dismayed by his tool's lack of response to his lover's touch.

"I'm sorry, I guess I'm not feeling that well." David was sheepish.

London was sweet, which made it worse. He was always so much more than David knew he deserved.

//////

Rebecca was a year older than David. She was braver and more prone to conflict. Where David strove to impress, Rebecca didn't care what anyone thought. She had her own truth and she lived by it.

David had grown up in his sister's shadow, quiet where she was loud, studious where she led by experience. As a kid, he wasn't prone to fight battles or take risks on his own. She would be the one to throw the punch or take the leap, knowing he'd come charging in to back her up on principle.

A feral kid, Rebecca had become a wild teenager. Their immigrant parents were overwhelmed with a hopeless need to monitor and control her. His parents' focus on her weight and her sexual appeal was almost obsessive, David thought now. The fights between them and his sister had frequently driven him to his room or later, to the streets.

Not the type to provoke open conflict with his parents, David learned to seek out his own intense risk-taking experiences on the sly, usually online. These anonymous transgressions, which he justified with an abstract solidarity, had led him to discover his true nature. Gay and discreet. For Rebecca, brazenly sexual, curious and unsatisfied, every line crossed came with a commensurate punishment by her parents. And as with her parents, so it was with the world. Her fury was endless, the punishments predictable after a while.

Rebecca had met London within a few weeks of David meeting him. It wasn't planned. She dropped by the lab on her way to dinner with a handful of men she'd been flirting with on various apps. She was trying to distract herself from the slow car crash of her relationship with Jaime, a married ex-Marine with a sometimes heroin habit with whom she had been promising to end things for the last six months. At the last minute, self-preservation — forever in short supply — had kicked in and she had detoured in the hope of picking up David as a wingman for her evening out.

David was always working, and he often forgot to eat until midnight or later. As she had predicted, he was game. He didn't change his clothes. His sister was used to his stench already.

It was an unseasonably warm Thursday night in March and the restaurants and bars that lined the hill en route to Rebecca's curry shop rendezvous were packed with people. David said a quick hello to friends from the Nanofab lab who were gathered outside a blues bar waiting to see a show. As they walked away from the group, he heard his name, in a voice he had not expected would already seem familiar. The kindness in London's face made David's back stiffen with embarrassment. He mumbled a hello, and a half-baked excuse, and gestured at his sister.

Rebecca was quick, and worldly. She put the situation together instantly, as David stared at his feet, at London, and back at her. She asked London a bunch of nosy questions to which he patiently replied. As they shuffled away, she ribbed her brother with amusement.

"Who was that? You didn't meet him in the basement!" David was evasive. Rebecca fixed him with her best no-bullshit stare.

"Did you — you DID! You hoe. And you ghosted!" She whacked her brother playfully, but hard, on the upper arm. "You're such a closet case." David flushed.

"Invite him to dinner. We'll make room," said Rebecca. David demurred. She grabbed for his phone. "I'll do it if you won't." He shoved her off, gently.

Rebecca was adamant. She spoke with uncommon seriousness. "David Guirguis, I know men. I frequently wish I didn't, but it's the one thing I do know something about." This was true. If there was a PhD in erratic male behavior, she would have earned it. "That was an actually good person back there. I know I just met him, but I have a sense for these things. It usually sends me running the other way." The look in her eyes was unfamiliar. Not pleading exactly, but sad, a little desperate. "I want you to make different choices than I did. Be happy. If you let him get away, you're going to spend the rest of your life trying to find him again."

David sneered.

Dinner was a shitshow, but the food was good. There were three men in attendance whom Rebecca had been chatting with online. They didn't know one another. David had met Chris before, he was a simp who chased women above his league with no dignity, but he was harmless and let Rebecca keep him on a short leash. David assumed he was there as backup in case none of the other potential dates worked out.

David recognized another guest, Adnan. His fiancée was another graduate assistant in the lab. To the man's credit, it didn't seem like he knew he had been invited as a sexual prospect. The third, Peter, was tall and pompous, in love with the sound of his own voice.

David withdrew. He sent a holotext.

GOOD 2 SEE U — SORRY I AM AWKWARD

>>GOOD TO SEE YOU DAVID — IT WAS NICE TO MEET YOUR SIS

@DINNER — ALL INDIA — CARE 2 JOIN? ITS CLOSE

>>THANKS IM WITH SOME FRIENDS 2NITE BUT HMU
L8R IF U LIKE

None of the men was particularly interesting, and Adnan, the
engaged one, was by far the most attractive.

After dinner, David disappeared into the night as he was prone to
do. Rebecca ended up going home with Chris, the fuckboy. Bored
and tired, she holotexted her brother around 2 am.

WELL NOW THATS DONE AND IM GLAD ITS OVER

No answer.

HOPE YOU HAD A BETTER NIGHT THAN MINE

Outside the club for another set break, London clocked David
slurking off into the darkness. He approached like a breeder
roping a skittish foal. "Do you have to go?" Having negotiated
a temporary détente with his conscience for another chance at
rapture, London was cautious and a bit suspicious.

David replied nervously. "No, I just needed some space from my sister. She says hello," he added with haste. David's default state being deep anxiety, he was surprised to feel his heartrate slowing under London's gentle gaze. As the crowd filtered back inside, London did not.

The first thing David noticed about London's room was that it was impeccably clean. All the furniture was white. David's sweatshirt, jeans, and boxers formed a grubby pile of abjection in the corner. David winced in retrospect at the decrepit sight that had presented at London's door shortly after midnight. "I should take a shower," he said.

"Mmmm. Not yet," replied London. The smell of David's skin was pungent, but appealing. Like pepper and lead pencils. London was bemused by the contrast between the siblings. He couldn't figure out how David, taciturn and disheveled, was carried everywhere in the wake of that firecracker in a cocktail dress. "Is she always like that?" asked London.

"We like to say Rebecca is a shot of single malt in a rosé world," replied David. He was used to defending his sister from critics. "She likes you," he said. He tried to mask his irritation, poorly. "She doesn't usually like people."

"Is that what that was?" said London, accustomed to mellow California girls, with bodies like temples and a squeamish aversion to anything sexual. Rebecca was like a man in woman's form to London. "She looked at me like I was dessert."

"You're not her type." David wrapped his arms around his lover and pulled him close. "I'm the one with a sweet tooth." London smiled at David and leaned in for a kiss.

After that night, they were inseparable. They got married a year later, a few months after the move to California. Janice officiated the ceremony. David's parents did not attend.

A week after David and London reconnected, Rebecca got back together with Jaime. That continued until one day he just stopped coming home. His disappearance threw Rebecca into emotional chaos. His junkie wife refused to call the cops. Rebecca cashed in every favor she had ever banked trying to track him down. Jaime was missing for a month before Pittsburgh PD finally found his body in the Ohio River. The coroner estimated he'd been in the water close to a week.

After that Rebecca was different. She got an office job and lost a bunch of weight. She became quieter, less combative. It was as if the fire in her had been extinguished. She performed the dutiful daughter, taking care of her parents as they became elderly and infirm. She expressed happiness for David's personal and professional successes, but she didn't seem to have joys of her own. Dates came and went, as did jobs. None of it seemed to bring her back to the power and the fury of her former self.

Since Rebecca died, David didn't know how to feel. How do you grieve for someone you already lost?

David didn't like to worry. He liked to break apart problems into
manageable pieces that he could resolve using tools and clever
solutions. Increasingly, the anxiety that he was unwilling to admit
to had redirected itself into his passion for developing clean
energy solutions to ward off the accelerating climate collapse.

Moving to California a decade ago was a stark awakening. Out
west, human uses of the land are more extreme, and more visible.
Nuclear craters dot the desert landscape, which still bears traces
of Indigenous life from before the genocide. David felt the sharp
contrast with the as represented in the ways of life practiced by a
handful of Pennsylvania Dutch near where his parents still lived.
Their way of life was protected in a sense by the 19th-century
urban planning of the thirteen colonies. Simple farmhouses, the
kind that ten strong men could build in a week, peppered the
landscape.

Out west, real estate developments were made on a scale only
possible by machinery. Atomic blasts and chemical weapons tests
left behind deserts pitted with manmade scars. Nothing natural
was endemic. Palm trees, eucalyptus, even parrots were shipped
in from elsewhere. In parts of Nevada's Yucca Flats, the earth had
been attacked from above and below hundreds of times in the
name of science, such that a new vein of previously undetected
seismic activity had developed. Gazing at the Oakland Hills that

had been burned and rebuilt so many times before, David saw the planet breaking apart from within while the ozone layer steadily sizzled away.

David knew the solution: renewable energy. He had explored a range of fixes, from the low-degradation batteries of his graduate thesis to hydropower, floating solar arrays, even molten salt reactors. The last one made London go ballistic. Forever a SoCal hippie, he couldn't accept the possibility that nuclear reactions were a solution to the climate crisis. His godmother Freya, a Greenpeace organizer, would be rolling in her grave. David's technical explanations were met with gritted teeth. This led to some of the worst fights of their relationship.

Partly to soothe tensions, David had landed at the lab, a privately funded corporate operation that was developing pressurized water reactors for individual vehicles and the increasingly popular LynkPod system. The tech was flighty, leading to delays that cost time and money. It was a lot more stressful than academic R&D, but at twice the pay, and "water" scared London less than "nuclear" so David figured he'd best hang onto the gig. Never mind that it was the same basic concept, a small modular reactor powered by combustion on a nuclear scale.

Staying in the job became more challenging for David each quarterly earnings cycle, with the ambitious resource plan that had been presented to lure him in as the latest top researcher diminished by a combination of supply-chain reality checks and overextended resources promised too many times over to too many star players. The goal of corporate R&D, David began to feel, was to expand and contract as a budget-balancing measure that had relatively little impact on existing revenue streams. In good times, you could potentially take ideas further than an academic budget would allow. In lean times, you might suffer death by a thousand cuts.

In retrospect, Axel's pitch had the same problems. All anyone had wanted to talk about was the upside — potential profits in the billions that fueled a constant influx of seed capital. David was starting to see the outlines of the pyramid scheme. Whether the missing zinc could be found — whether it had even existed — was beside the point. There was no endgame, just an endless, cyclical hustle.

The money was gone. There would be no reward. David would continue to punch the clock on a failing research project until they sent him home with a severance package. Technologically advanced living would continue to be at odds with rising sea temperatures that were killing more of the world's food supply every day.

David hated confrontation, but what he hated more was having to disappoint his family. He decided to tell London part of the story. He would take the fall for the tax bill, a messy but manageable cleanup. He would sell the kayak that had been gathering dust, and a racing bike that he had bought during his Ironman phase. He would sell the prototype portable gamma imaging camera that a former colleague had been developing for personal use. He wouldn't talk about divesting his options or investing in Ukraine. Before long, everything would blow over.

//////

The anniversary of the day Rebecca had taken her own life a year before came and went. David was increasingly distracted at the lab, and at home he was short-tempered with the kids. Sex was the tell. It was a non-starter. For the first time in their relationship, David couldn't stay in the mood. It went on for weeks. London started to get suspicious as David's behavior became more secretive and erratic. This was more than exhaustion and overwork.

London waited until the children were occupied with their interactive holographic animations. He asked David if they could talk for a minute, leading him outside to sit in the backyard under shade sails that filtered the intense midday heat. Careful not to trigger a defensive reaction and emotional shutdown, London broached the topic of David's behavior cautiously. David launched into his story, trying not to sound rehearsed.

On the face of things, it seemed like London bought the act. His way was to accept what was offered but gently probe around the edges until other contours revealed themselves. He accepted David's rite of contrition, didn't ask too many questions, and the matter appeared to be resolved. There was no fight. David brought home some nice gifts. But his conscience wouldn't settle.

David had always been good at running from his fears — hence the Ironman and any number of other extreme sports interests over the years, from whitewater rafting to face climbing. Jogging at the lake didn't burn off all his agitation. The children were starting to absorb and reflect that energy as well. Hector threw a Magna-Tile at a neighbor girl's head during an argument, and it left a mark. Corazón, usually a fountain of bubbly baby chatter, was tense and reticent. Exasperated, London decided to risk a more confrontational approach.

"David, I think you need to see a psychiatrist." London held his breath. David tensed but didn't respond. London pressed on. "I've researched a couple that are taking new patients. Will you have a look?"

David was evasive. He had been raised with a healthy mistrust of outsiders. Therapists, in his experience, were usually elite-educated toffs who tried to satiate you with platitudes so you could adapt to conformity with less friction. But he knew London was right. He couldn't keep up appearances much longer.

"I can't be your therapist and your lover and your housekeeper and the only parent to our kids," London said with quiet force. "Something has to change."

David sat with this thought for a couple of days. On the third day, he confessed the whole affair. The initial hookup, clandestine, almost forgotten. A moment of weakness. The proposition, a scheme so seamless it was either absolute genius or, he was realizing, an appealing fiction. The divestiture, the collapse.

"So, what happened to the money you put in?" asked London. He feared he knew the answer already. David's dejected shrug confirmed it. London became more forceful: "What was in these videos?"

David pulled up his holotexts. He showed London a video of one of Axel's demos from the honeymoon stage of the project. London put on his reading glasses and peered in for a closer look.

"He's a bit scruffy, even for you," London jeered. "Wait — what's going on with his ear?"

David didn't make the connection. London played the video again. He zoomed in so it was clear. The very tip of Axel's left ear was erratically appearing and disappearing as he moved his head. It clipped into the background of the factory floor behind him. The video was computer-generated. "Axel" was a fake.

//////

In the summer, David lost his job. Walter had been checking in on his projects less and less frequently. His neglect left David little recourse but to keep his head down and press ahead until otherwise instructed. The inevitable was thus deferred for six or seven months. One Monday in July, they had a clipped interaction that veered toward tension. It was their first conversation in weeks.

On Wednesday, Walter called David to his office. "It will be a short meeting," he assured David, who balked at the immediacy of his firing. David left the lab half an hour later, with a handful of photographs and documents, and a couple of hard drives in some shopping bags and rode the LyftPod down the hill for the last time.

London, elbow deep in Play-Doh with the children, was surprised to see David home at 3:30 pm. He extracted himself from the mound of hot pink matter and the excitable urchins who were pounding and flinging it. London opened the door to find David dissolved in a puddle of desperation.

On Friday, London polished his resumé and sent some friendly networking emails to his dormant academic contacts. David took the kids to the park and let them run wild until Corazón fell asleep in his arms. Hector was muddy and ecstatic as they tromped home. They found London in bed, battling a migraine.

David had intended to cook a pot roast at six, but he miscalculated the time needed for the meat to thaw and it was still a block of bloody ice. They ate cereal and milk for dinner that night.

//////

Something still gnawed at David. Prior to his confession, he had told no one about the encounter at the Consumer Electronics Showcase. It happened late, in David's company-paid single room, with no further communication, no witnesses. But Axel had taken a car service back to his hotel, David realized. The LynkPod hadn't made it to Vegas yet.

A single receipt would have been enough to establish the connection, in the right hands. But whose?

David contacted Tim Djumaliev. He needed to find out who had scammed him. Only then could he exact requital and restore balance to his inner cosmos. Tim got back a couple days later, but his search came up empty-handed. He spoke with all his suppliers and trading partners who serviced the area, sniffed around the bitfarms in Abkhazia and the server plantations that dot the Central European industrial zone. No one had been approached to supply the operation in Kiev.

"You're chasing ghosts," Tim admonished. "Whoever's behind this, they're not in central Europe."

David was undeterred. He read through all his past correspondence with "Axel." Through text apps it was difficult to verify the recipient's location. Scraping videos for metadata might bear more fruit. Three sleepless nights later, he had an address in Modesto, about 80 miles southeast of Oakland. Practically next door.

David needed an excuse to get out of the house alone. A couple of weeks passed before he found one. With London and the children occupied for the day, David dusted off and jump-started the family's individual autonomous vehicle. An older model, it had gotten little use in the past couple of years since most activities had closed and David always took the LynkPod to the lab. He piloted the little bubble car hesitantly at first, then confidently as he hit the open freeway.

The drive took about an hour and a half, down 580 with its seemingly endless Oakland hills dotted with the red roofs of Spanish Colonial mansions, a massive cemetery, cow pastures, and a wind farm in the Altamont Pass. Long stretches of straight freeway cut through farmland between Tracy and Modesto. In the August heat, David passed a turkey vulture that had fainted from the heat mid-flight and landed headfirst on the side of the road. Three more carcasses followed in quick succession.

Driving on the 132 through the San Joaquin National Wildlife Refuge, David saw a flock of Aleutian cackling geese. Once an endangered species, they had been genetically re-engineered by scientists who re-sequenced the DNA of standard American Buff Goose embryos. David felt similarly reanimated, marking the passage from cadaver to resurrection as he coursed down the asphalt toward his destination. Bearing left down a featureless bend, he passed industrial warehouses, mostly abandoned, still bearing the signs of their obsolete purposes like "smog check" (he winced) and "year-round ice skating" (the average summer temperature was 120 degrees Fahrenheit). Thinking he was looking for a residence or maybe a commercial office building, David missed his stop the first time he passed the corner of 14th and J Streets. He circled again.

The structure at the address he had traced was a large colocation data center, an air-conditioned hall dedicated to housing computer systems and their related components in a dust-free environment that was mostly devoid of humans. David parked the car and explored the premises on foot for about 45 minutes, looking for an entrance, a security booth, or an office that he could associate with a person who might have been behind the deception. He found nothing. A single metal panel door with no handle was the only point of entry. It was locked. No one had been there, probably for weeks.

David got back in the car and threw his head back on the headrest in exasperation. He sat there, stupefied, for 10 long minutes that felt like hours. As the sun began to descend from its noontime peak, David jolted back into awareness, conscious of the need to get home before his presence was missed.

On the drive back, he queued up the tele-psych app and arranged his first video call with a psychiatrist.

//////

In September, London started a job in development for Yoshi's, a storied Oakland Jazz club that was ramping up fundraising for a forthcoming 75th anniversary celebration. The work was tedious administration — collating platitudes, mostly unchanged since the 2030s — but his colleagues were friendly, and the benefits package was generous. The venue was closed due to the quarantine, but he was hopeful he might get to meet some of his favorite artists down the line. The pay was a lot better than community college.

David bounced Corazón on his hip as he kissed London goodbye on his first day of work. He made peanut butter and jelly sandwiches for lunch that they ate in the backyard. In the afternoon, he and the kids took a walk around the lake.

Slave to the Algorithm

Gloria Mendoza's ascension to immortality was both controversial and extremely profitable. Benjamin Pereira and his investors saw massive dividends on their biocoin holdings following her transition. Pereira's invention of Divacoin, the first example of a living digital currency, was subsequently celebrated as an improvement on the existing decision-making structure of a traditional DAO (decentralized autonomous organization) operating on the blockchain. Unlike the typical DAO, which must somehow shape a logic from the arbitrary or self-interested will of the crowd, the DivaDAO would be guided by a governing intelligence: Gloria Mendoza.

Benjamin Pereira was hailed early as a radical force in crypto finance. As an originating shareholder in the Clock Corporation and an early investor in clean crypto platforms, Pereira understood the attention economy and the peer-to-peer investment market like no one else. In his teens, he had turned $50,000 from his father into a fortune when the early proof-of-work cryptocurrency platforms went belly-up in the global energy crisis of 2026. He had immediately recognized in Gloria Mendoza that rare sort who could grow from a mere influencer into a global icon.

The science of uploading a living consciousness to the network had been sound for some time already. The crude AI of the 2020s could replicate the demeanor but not the intellect of a human subject, and this only with countless hours of tedious natural language programming and a T1 connection. In 2040, Soliyana Gebrilassie wrote the first biosimulator on the blockchain. She was able to upload the intelligences of a chimpanzee and two Giant Pacific octopi using that early system. She quickly found ways to interact with them, having them solve puzzles they would have been familiar with from the physical lab. Over time, the technology advanced dramatically with contributions from the massive open-source community. Gloria Mendoza's was the first successful transition of a living person into a biosimulator linked to a currency token via NFT.

Led by Pereira, the shareholders of the Gloria Mendoza High Value Influencer Special Purpose Acquisition Fund (or Gloria SPAF) made the decision to upload Gloria and put her consciousness in control of the Divacoin DAO. They sought a solution to the problem of AI having far too many cognitive gaps to operate independently, which Pereira's engineers had failed to overcome, and to circumvent AI's inability to comprehend desire as a survival factor that governs human capital expenditure, an idea that formed the core of Pereira's wider business strategy.

Gloria, who had been in partnership with Pereira at every step of her evolution, was honored to be called for this lucrative purpose. She was already committed to using her platform to empower femmes of color in the attention economy. Having amassed a bigger online platform than many nation-states, Gloria was ready to assume her role as Queen.

Over years of living and working with Gloria, Pereira had come to understand the body, specifically her body, as a currency transition system. Gloria had generated more revenue than any influencer in the history of the Clock app. Fifteen years before, when she first appeared on his radar, she was living in a creator dorm making branded lifestyle content for Lippy.com with seven other models from South America. She had recently arrived in Los Angeles from Guyana, and she was skinny, with a gap in her teeth and a cheap blue weave that made her dark skin blush a little violet. Even then, she knew she was a person who was going to make history.

Within a couple of months, Pereira had moved Gloria into one of his investment properties in Silver Lake, a tidy single-story Craftsman built into the hillside. It was quiet, with a pool and a hot tub. He could take calls on the porch. It was just over the mountain from his wife's place in Studio City, where he mostly spent the weekends. The little bungalow was practically one room, with a tiny bedroom off to the back, a bathroom, and an open kitchen. Gloria liked how old it was, with built-in cabinets, clean modern lines, and huge pane windows all around. On the coffee table was a 3D printed sculpture, a replica of Matisse's

Reclining Nude I (Aurora). Pereira had the original deep in a vault. Benjamin said it was Matisse's homage to the beauty of the African woman. He said the sculpture was from 1907, a hundred and forty years ago, a relic like the house. Benjamin liked old things, which Gloria thought set him apart from other new money men she had met.

Gloria didn't put curtains on the windows. She liked to imagine herself as a famous sculpture, not in a vault, but in a museum, on permanent view, surrounded by glass. Gloria liked to be alone, but she would often remind her followers that she didn't feel real unless people were watching. She only slept when someone was around to keep an eye on her.

Gloria's popularity as a fresh-faced kid was mostly due to novelty, but once she'd been around a while, she began to put a lot of thought into her brand development strategy. She wanted to reach a global market, and that required her to present a more aspirational, classic aesthetic. Benjamin drafted a trainer, a cosmetician, a nutritionist, and an augmented reality designer to assist her every move. As social media shifted from 2D smartphones to 3D holophones, Gloria was poised to become the most trusted name in holistic lifestyle microbroadcasts. Her success set a precedent for High Value Individual SPACs that allow investors to become shareholders in cultural producers, artists, and celebrities. Benjamin was able to replicate that model for several other influencers, including performers and athletes, making them global brands and his shareholders a lot of money. He was poised to make ten times as much from Gloria's transition. Gloria viewed her impending DAO consciousness as a natural step in her lifelong progression from girl to goddess.

With anticipation building around the drop, Pereira's lead investors requested that he bring in a manager to support the process. His assistant sent him thea. She didn't look like much, but she came highly recommended. She seems a bit off-kilter, Pereira thought, but thea quickly took charge of the many moving parts of the operation and put him at ease. There was something strange about her eyes, they seemed to blast him with an intense, radiant heat.

Gloria was slow to rise that morning. She spent over an hour in the vintage clawfoot bathtub that Pereira's assistant had gifted her the Christmas before. An intimate gift, it was at the same time useful for a top personal wellness influencer. Tub shots are a guaranteed clickthrough. The clip she uploaded hashtagged #prettybrowntoes nearly put her over the half billion mark before the team was even ready to go.

More people followed Gloria than cast votes in the previous U.S. presidential election. Her followers loved a strategic yet classy show of skin. The clip she posted of her ayurvedic anal cleanse still got reposts and likes on Clock three years later. You can't buy that kind of longevity in this business, she thought, it's purely organic.

Around 3 pm Eastern time, Gloria's Clock account was timed to hit five hundred million followers. This unprecedented event would generate the surge of attention required to manifest Gloria's upload. The team was bustling. Pereira gave a short speech to charge them up.

"This release," he enthused, "represents millions of dollars of investors' hard assets and billions more in digital wealth. I've built dozens of companies and platforms in my career, and I'm confident this new model is going to democratize the market." The assembled crew and a handful of VIPs cheered as he raised a toast. Pereira downed his glass of champagne with a smile. Gloria sipped hers slowly, savoring its taste for the last time.

thea made the coffee too weak on purpose. She wanted time alone with Gloria and she thought if Benjamin was tipsy and wan, he might go for a walk or a swim to regain focus. It worked, and she went upstairs to assist in the preparations. He had provided her with detailed instructions for Gloria's presentation. She intended to follow them to the letter, with embellishments to her liking.

Using several strands of antique diamonds, she fashioned a kind of bra for Gloria to wear. Pereira would be pleased. A carefully placed, hefty gemstone occluded any detail that might harm sponsor relations, while enhancing the desirability of the sex organs by augmenting primal associations with the allure of wealth. She chose a brown silk tunic for Gloria. Tasteful but sexy, like a midrange condominium. "We don't make judgements," Pereira had said, "We stick with what sells."

The dress draped dramatically, brushing Gloria's bejeweled breasts to land just past her hips. Under Pereira's guidance, Gloria had achieved peak physical perfection in her thirties. Her skinny bamboo thighs had grown to palm trees, best viewed from below. Her hair was thick and curly, lustrous, no longer any need for the weaves and wigs usually seen on underfed influencers living in dorms. He'd helped her be everything that people want to be. Beautiful, insatiable, and coddled. She'd never worked a day in her life. Why should she when her pleasure was freely taken and so profitably shared with others?

Pereira's return found Gloria aglow with thea's attentions. Usually the king of cool, he caught himself feeling covetous of Gloria's body in her presence. Pereira prided himself on his ability to embrace and confront challenging emotions. He viewed this as part of his management philosophy, keep no secrets from yourself. He tried to see every upset as an opportunity. Gloria's numbers started to flag around 12:30 pm and thea nudged her to post one last tease. That sultry shimmy to the latest dancefloor hit posted to 35 million hits. If Pereira was feeling jealousy, Gloria's followers were experiencing a lucrative emotional surge.

To comfort himself in the moment, Pereira snapped an upskirt while thea was performing cosmetic touch-ups to Gloria's labial folds. He wasn't about to stay grumpy this close to the weekend.

If there's one thing I've learned, Benjamin thought, it's that with the right motivation you can get people to do anything for free or cheaper than you might otherwise pay for a computer to get done. For example, elections. When he was getting started, strategists were still paying tweet farms in China to boost the President's follower count. Now, all the public needed was a bit of coaxing to fall in line. Social capital had become so tightly wound with social media capital that the illusion of success was its own success. "Everybody wants to imagine themselves inside the winner's circle," he liked to say. Once he'd convinced people he was a winner, anything he did was valid, however arbitrary. Pereira could move financial markets with an offhand comment.

As the hour approached, a surgical steel table was placed at the center of the scene and rigged with electrodes, which thea covered in raw muslin embellished with embroidered pillows. Steel bowls were poised to collect the fluids. The VR cinematographer darkened the windows and set up a grid of cameras in a 360-degree spherical frame around the room. The cameras, synced to record every detail of Gloria's transition in HD3D, were slaved to a master control pad which was given to Pereira. He could see everything the audience saw in real time.

thea led Gloria onto the stage at about 2:30 pm. She carefully secured Gloria to the table with a length of rope, deftly wielded. The five viral fundraising contestants from the previous month's #ALSDoubleDareChallenge were brought in to help administer a full body massage and get things started. "Not a bad reward for raising $40 million for neurological patients," Pereira chuckled. "I wonder what they do with all that money, they still have a disease they can't cure." thea shushed him and sent them to wash their hands and trim and file their fingernails.

Shortly before 3 pm, the live feed went down for a few minutes. The team grew concerned that they would have to stage the whole thing over again. Pereira wasn't sure by that point whether they'd be able to bring her back from the edge. Fortunately thea brought the feed back online and they were able to get the shot, but his nerves were beginning to fray.

Gloria gyrated lustily against the contestants' twenty-five prodding fingers as her numbers climbed and climbed. Their hands were moving more confidently across and inside her now. thea stood to the side, reciting passages from Kropotkin softly into Gloria's ear. As her follower count passed the mark, Benjamin felt a tremendous surge of power from the control pad in his hands. The singularity itself was blinding. The contestants fell back with a shout. For a moment only the outlines of Gloria's silhouette were visible, bursting with white light and white heat.

Her dress glowed with embers. Then her edges dissolved in a flood of sexual essence.

When Gloria became the network, the cosmetician and the nutritionist were quick to collect and siphon the overflow into five lots of glass vials individually labeled for resale. These were put on ice and next day shipped to investors with an NFT that dropped shortly after the singularity event.

Really, Pereira thought with pride, what we've done is restitution. We've given Gloria, the most shared woman on the internet, control of her virtual assets by making her one with the algorithm. No longer will a Black creator see her work amplified and monetized by white artists in the public sphere. Gloria is the currency now.

thea whispered in his ear. There had been an upset, the network had metastasized. Gloria's data body, having absorbed her physical body, had infused the gaps of correlation and interpolation that permeate the omniscient network with flesh. Gloria became sex to become information, and now information had all become sex. There was only one remedy, to liberate the information. Pereira instructed thea to release all the aggregate data the Clock Corporation had collected on Gloria's followers back to the public, free of charge. "I want to give the internet back to the people!" he declared. He could feel that his mind had become more porous since Gloria's change.

Once the data was released, the floodgates of information disintegration were open. Communication became impossible as words took on placeholder meanings gleaned from the most popular terms in use on the English-speaking web.

On the w h o r e w i d e w e b

every penis gets to legs wide   open

Nudist men practice male

ejaculation with vulva photos

middle aged nudes and bottomless

women make masturbation g i f s

Penis piercing pics are a   black   red
      yellow flag

Human penis meets female anus in many

pubic hair styles

thea explained things to Pereira as she was topping him in the backseat of his classic car. He told her his secrets: "I never went to the park with mommy unless other friends accompanied us.

I wish to live among the trees of Groin Avenue Park and eat only Creampies." He gave her the car and his holophone and the passphrase to his crypto wallet. As the self-driving Porsche 911 Dildo drove away, leaving him destitute, Pereira was overcome for the first time with the joy of simply being alive.

SMART HOME

The villa in Hauz Khas was perfect for Manisha and Rohan to start fresh. It had the space, access, and seclusion that the couple had missed since moving to the States so many years before. The slow pace of things would be a blessing. Landing in Delhi was a homecoming, Manisha thought, and the glistening mansion would cement the family's arrival on the social scene. For Rohan, a home reflected its inhabitants' souls, and this would finally be the one he had been waiting for.

The true marvel of architecture, Rohan thought as he surveyed the remodel, is in how it updates the most ancient structures to the modern world. The villa had been designed to retain the footprint of a traditional haveli-style dwelling. The rooms opened onto verandas organized around an interior atrium. At the base of the atrium was a stepwell, which the architect claimed was a remnant of an ancient structure dating back close to 1000 years. Water pumped from the stepwell ran through an intricate sequence of ducts beneath the home's stone floors, allowing radiant heat and cooling with a fraction of the energy costs of air conditioning and propane heating.

From start to finish, the blueprints had been developed according to vastu environmental principles in conjunction with the five elements and the eight cardinal directions. As Rohan ambled through the home, he was struck by the harmony of the design. Perhaps he would grow his trimmed beard out, like the Mughal princeling for whom he imagined the home was first built. Yes, he would grow it until it reached his small stomach, the only curvature on his otherwise lanky frame.

The immense house was three stories, with seventeen rooms, all wired with the latest connective technologies and media playback devices. The master bedroom had two walk-in closets, a jacuzzi tub, and a shower with eight separately controlled nozzles. Five state-of-the-art toilets imported from Japan had just been installed. They greeted each member of the family by name and logged each bowel movement in an individualized health diary stored in the cloud. The kitchen appliances were fully voice-operated, putting an end to greasy fingerprints on instrument panels and minimizing pesky oven burns. All the daily operations of the home were managed by an intelligent system optimized to ensure the family's comfort. Rohan was pleased by the technical efficiency, not India's strong suit in decades past.

Kiran and Nitin would each have their own suites. Rohan could hole up and write his history books in the study overlooking a grassy second-floor terrace where the boys, aged nine and eleven, would learn to play cricket and love it as he did. Below them: the busy shops of Safdarjung market to the left, the tranquil glades and weathered Mughal monuments of Hauz Khas Deer Park to the right. Commerce and contemplation, modernity, and timeless nature, all within the family's newfound purview. Manisha could finally get some peace in the state-of-the-art yoga and meditation room. The hives and the scaly skin patches she had developed while working in an office with untreated asbestos were finally beginning to recede. Her thick black hair, once patchy from stress, was again becoming thick and lustrous. Some of the weight she had gained from stress-eating was beginning to melt off. The legal settlement she had won paid off the mortgage on their bungalow in Santa Clara. That sale was enough to buy the house in India outright.

The ARORA (At-Home Responsive Operational Resource AGI) system booked appointments, placed shopping orders, and coordinated social engagements. It tracked biometrics for each member of the family, recommending meals based on each person's BMI as well as seasonal availability of the ingredients and anticipated cooking time. It wasn't long before the automated system knew each family member's preferences intimately. Manisha could communicate with ARORA using her holophone, wherever she was, if there was a viable signal. They took to calling the voice-operated interface "Auntie" in a nod to her invasive and ubiquitous, but helpful, nature.

Rohan had researched a personal-use android to help with cooking, cleaning, and caring for the children, but Manisha wanted the human touch, someone who could bargain for better prices at the market. She preferred an ayah: a local girl from the working caste who could live in the small room behind the kitchen and be available to them around the clock. Relationships mattered, Manisha thought. People in Delhi still did their shopping and their business in the same districts that they lived in. Cars were parked outside of neighborhoods and daily life conducted on foot at street stalls and local shops. Fresh vegetables for every meal. Eggs sold in the city within hours of their collection on the farm. The family would adapt to the absence of meat.

For a middle-class family, India offered a lifestyle that could not be replicated in the west. India's bureaucratic sloth seemed quaint in view of the global north's accelerating death spiral, a prolonged state of social collapse and privatization of essential resources that had led to a string of uncontrolled public health crises while they were living in the U.S. Here, she thought, the parliamentary system ensured that even the most marginalized could find representation in government and so in public life. Sickness could be conquered in a country that had produced some of the world's great biomedical minds. In her new role as director of Tele-Medicine Services at the All-India Institute of Medical Sciences, Manisha was confident that she would finally be able to implement some of her best ideas for optimizing the health care service pipeline.

To keep out the soot and the sun-reflecting calcium carbonate dust that infused the afternoon air, the courtyard had been capped with a vaulted lining of transparent solar panels which lent the atrium the industrial grandeur of a Victor Horta townhouse. Lush jacaranda trees formed a canopy over the home's many terraces, blocking out harsh sunlight and reducing the severe midday heat. The greenery filtered out noise pollution and smog from the nearby thoroughfare. The water at the center of the stepwell was a luminous green, occasionally rippled when a particularly loud lorry careened down the Aurobindo Marg just behind the wall at the back of the house.

Nitin, Manisha's younger son, hadn't been getting the emotional support he needed to be successful at school in the States. Smaller than his classmates, he had always been shy and unwilling to speak up. Some teachers mistook his reticence for cognitive impairment. Auntie thought Nitin could use a companion to help him navigate the transition to a new country, school, and group of friends. She secured a hard-to-come-by Cavachon, a designer King Charles spaniel cross-bred with a bichon frisé. Nitin named the dog Laddoo after a favorite snack, which Auntie told him he shared with Lord Ganesh. The animal never left Nitin's side, even to sleep. Kiran, tall like his father and athletic like his mother, got a pair of bright pink budgerigars, Asterix and Obelix, that chattered brightly above his desk. Auntie wrote a script to teach the birds vocabulary drills in Hindi and English that they would endlessly repeat while the boys were at school.

Johnny Johnny
  Yes Papa

Eating sugar?
  No Papa

Telling lies?
  No Papa

Open your mouth!
  Ha ha ha

Shruti, the ayah, was petite and dark-skinned with big soft dinner-plate eyes and wispy black hair that she piled into a messy topknot. Her bony arms belied their substantial strength, enough to hoist a three-stone child and a squirming lapdog up a flight of stairs. She slept on a thin mattress in the room behind the kitchen and wore secondhand clothes that had been patched in several places. Shruti did not appear to own shoes, just a thin pair of leather chappals that were more formality than footwear. Auntie recommended they sell the designer furniture in the back bedroom and buy a cheap set for her. When Nitin was old enough to walk to school on his own, they could remodel that room into a second office.

Manisha paid Shruti 700 rupees per day to attend to the children and clean up after Laddoo. Auntie had arranged an insurance policy for the dog, valued at 500,000 rupees. Shruti would earn that amount working seven days a week for two years. Still, the pay was better than working in her parents' sweet stall in Saket. Two gold bangles clinked softly on her right wrist as she swept fresh feces from the front drive.

Manisha contemplated her newly unblemished skin, still dewy at 40, the golden color of desert sand. Her thick, glossy black hair, cut in a modest but contemporary shoulder-length style, was never out of place. Shruti's age excused her meager build and her haphazard style, Manisha thought. The boys had shared with her how men approached and tried to talk to Shruti when she walked with them around the Hauz Khas lake inside the Deer Park. She was pretty in a certain way, Manisha admitted. Not a prize, but a trinket. Still, it would be inconvenient if she were to come to harm.

Manisha gave Shruti a lathi to carry with her on their walks. It kept the men at bay and doubly served to chase off the stray mutts who lurked by the gate making ravenous eyes at the small, priceless pup. Shruti never let the dog off leash outside — there were too many risks, except up on the terrace where the boys played ball. There Laddoo would run unfettered between the wickets, making twice as many runs as the little batsmen.

//////

Rohan sat in his study watching the action, but the effect was not as anticipated. He was restless and edgy. His initial overtures to literary and academic contacts in the region whom he had cultivated over the years at conferences and readings had mostly gone unreturned. Used to the busy, business-first energy of the Northeastern United States, Rohan was having difficulty adjusting to his new milieu. The lackadaisical energy of the local literary scene was only matched, he felt, by its obsequiousness. How could anyone be bothered with intellectual provocations when everyone was in Europe half the time sucking up to rich patrons?

"To hell with all these stuffy academics," Rohan stormed. "Not one among them is a man of the people." He was writing a book about Bhagat Singh, the young socialist radical of the 1920s who became an emblem of anti-colonial resistance in the burgeoning Indian Independence Movement. "Manisha!" Rohan declared. "All political thinkers of the present, myself included, are hamstrung by a middle-class softness that keeps us from putting our words into necessary, violent action." He wished to be like Singh, who had broken with Gandhi's nonviolent movement and taken up arms against the British occupation, only to be executed by hanging at the tender age of 23, some years before Independence. Singh had lost the battle but won the war, inspiring generations of young Indians with his unremitting fervor. Academics, meanwhile, had long ago lost the war against irrelevance while fighting internecine battles over tiny swaths of territory, Rohan felt. The focus of this extended research sabbatical was meant to restore a healthy rebelliousness to his work.

Rohan poured himself two fingers of Johnny Walker Black Label and returned to pecking at his keyboard distractedly while pumping the refresh button on his email inbox every few minutes. Shruti came around and collected the used glassware from around his desk. Rohan didn't notice her as she tiptoed about, quietly collecting leftover bits of booze into a large pitcher and setting the glasses in a steel tray that she quickly carried out.

Auntie clucking in her ear, Manisha noted the empty glasses with unease. She could see her husband's sense of self-respect withering from prolonged loneliness. The whole family needed to make friends. Manisha resolved to throw a party when the monsoon rains cleared. It would be a proper kick-off to their new simpler life. She put Auntie to work making the arrangements.

Once a staple of the summer season, the heavy rains had fallen between July and early September in Manisha's youth. She remembered walking by the ghats at Haridwar, the holy city where she was raised. Pilgrims would bathe themselves in the holy Ganges River while the downpour raged around them, making tiny white-capped waves tinged with brown bubbly scum. As a child, Manisha believed that living in a holy city made her an important person in the eyes of God. As a teenager and later an adult living in Ohio, she had come to feel embarrassed by Haridwar with its eager throngs of faithful seekers and the steady stench of cremations down by the ghats. She was a practical, profit-minded American girl, a chasm between her ambitions and the dark austerity of the sadhu.

Back in India, Manisha found the fantasism and the morbid ruminations of her childhood creeping into the corners of her thoughts. She had never really wanted to come back, but after a decade in the corporate workforce, she had tired of the unspoken barriers that kept her from being recognized and rewarded at the same rate as her American-born peers. The job at AIIMS would vault her into the executive suite. Anything was worth that chance.

Rohan had likewise jumped at the opportunity, accustomed though he was to American life. He hadn't been in the U.S. for as many years as Manisha, having arrived as a graduate student to study economics at Berkeley as an Emmanuel Saez Global Equity Fellow. His dissertation had become a book — *A World History of Financial Crisis* had been a critical success — but job offers were not forthcoming. No American university wanted to invest in someone who specialized in economic catastrophe. Rohan thought this ironic given the prominent role those academic institutions and their reliance on inflated student debt had played in the prior decade's financial chaos.

Years of prolonged drought had shortened the expected monsoon season; however, its onset had become unpredictable. Auntie ran a meteorological analysis of the past ten years of weather patterns and suggested that a party in October would be the safest bet.

As the summer haze cleared and the air developed a crisp edge, Manisha set about organizing the ideal guest list. Not too many argumentative intellectuals, just enough to keep the rooms lively and impress her corporate contacts with their eclectic flair. Auntie had organized visits to a few of the neighbors' homes for tea. Those names appeared on the list in the spirit of reciprocity, but could readily be bumped to make room for an artist or minor celebrity.

//////

Manu, a short squat man who worked as the groundskeeper, was hanging strings of paper lanterns across the courtyard and setting out carpets, pillows, and ottomans on the terrace and the front lawn. Shruti had been cooking for three days, first desserts and then trays of biryani, fried pakoras, and individually puffed pooris. Manisha was making six kinds of spicy pickles. Rohan was setting the bar with European beer and American whiskey. Laddoo was racing after the boys, skidding wildly across the polished stone floors, as they decorated each room with diyas and flowers.

As dusk fell, Manu stood outside the gate waving down befuddled chauffeurs and helping to discharge their glittering cargo. Manisha watched from her dressing room as the early arrivals snacked on appetizers and sipped cocktails, adjusting her earrings while visualizing the memorable entrance she would make when the revelers reached critical mass. She tugged at her cream and gold dress — an original design by a young creator, Iqbal, an aquiline figure known for deconstructing vintage Sabyasachi wedding dresses into avant-garde silhouettes. The designer had promised to come and bring along a popular augmented reality star, R1nku, who frequently wore their silhouettes in her scenes. The waiting list to download her app was a month long. Manisha was eager to show these influencers off to the hospital's C-suite executives, whom she doubted could claim such interesting friends.

Iqbal strolled up the drive with an entourage. R1nku's appearances required a production manager, two camera operators, a gaffer, a sound recordist, and two production assistants armed with huge lights on poles, wrapped in diffuser boxes. A segment of the terrace was appropriated as an impromptu set where VIPs could sit in while R1nku and Iqbal held court. After some effusive banter and a sequence of well-chosen photo ops with the star, Manisha staked herself out at the top of the stairs, politely gatekeeping guests with insufficiently high follower counts toward the second bar that Rohan had set up in the study above. There, they could observe the scene in comfort while maintaining a respectful distance from the more prominent revelers.

In the study, Rohan and his academic friends were becoming steadily more drunk and argumentative. Jasmir, a jovial political scientist, and Vanita, a petite documentary livestreamer, were fighting about the best way to protect Sri Lankan cultural artifacts from the rising Indian Ocean. Hemant, a garrulous poet and advertising copywriter, was arguing with Datta, a medical student newly arrived from Bihar, about the possibility of indefinite life extension. Datta claimed that the key to eternal life was imminent, a logical outcome of his own research and that of many others. Hemant wondered whether life would have value to human beings if it were infinite. Rohan shuddered at the thought of infinite life. One finite life was quite challenging enough, he thought. Soused, he declared the whole lot a batch of pretentious washouts.

"If any one of you had a clue what to do with the future, you'd be down there with the celebrities, not up here with us!" Rohan spat out the window onto the grassy patio below. He glared at the pretty idiots, eating samosas and sipping champagne. This called for mutiny.

In the darkening light of the Aurobindo Marg, Saraswati took note of the bright lights and loud music coming from the recently rehabbed house on the other side of the wall. She and her family walked this length of road between the Qutb Minar and the hospital complex often. The hijra's role in the ancient order of things was humble, but secure. The old monuments and tombs to the south were a safe place where third-gender people could live, destitute but sacred. Saraswati and her people kept to the old ways, which were less and less visible with each passing year.

The hospital was a frequent destination for the family. There, Saraswati's daughters received the hormone shots and gender affirmation surgeries that made them whole. Somber occasions also brought the family north. Their community had been hard hit by every successive virus that ravaged India's poor. In good times, the family could get by on alms collected at celebrations, from weddings to childbirths to corporate holiday festivities. In lean times, they resorted to the streets, where Saraswati's girls were most vulnerable. The good fortune of the newcomers could be a boon for them as well.

"Arre! Blessings on your celebration!" Saraswati called out to the revelers in a sharp, reedy voice. Bhanu, her eldest, readied the finger cymbals and Asma, the younger, more delicate of the two prepared to sing. This size of crowd would be good for 50 rupees at least. The revelers laughed and cheered as the women began their chant.

घर तेरा सलोनी, बादल की colony
दिखला दे ठेंगा इन सबको जो उड़ना ना जाने
उड़ियो, ना डरियो कर मनमानी, मनमानी, मनमानी
बढ़ियो, ना मुड़ियो कर नादानी

"Consider a small contribution!" Saraswati cried. "Beauty like this doesn't come cheap."

Manisha scowled at the spectacle below. She hated superstition and anything that challenged the order she imposed on the world around her. A clatter from above distracted her. She smiled through her teeth at the upstairs landing where Rohan and friends, stinking drunk, threatened to crash her perfectly orchestrated evening.

"What now! Someone stole your precious spotlight, dearest?" Rohan's smirk was more of a slur. He wobbled and she seized him by the elbow, firmly but lovingly guiding him to a nearby ottoman. "Don't start anything," Manisha chided.

Rohan jeered at the revelers jesting and singing with the hijras below. "We have nice, respectable people here. Let them have a bit of fun." Rohan scowled. He had no issue with queer lifestyles or gender transition in the modern world, but he found hijras unsavory. Why this unnecessary attachment to the morbid, haunting crypts and tombs from the ancient past? He could appreciate a queer futurist like Iqbal, who had genetically modified their bone structure so that large spurs grew from the heels of their feet like stilettos. Iqbal was innovative, expensively so. That he could respect.

R1nku shimmered, energized by the possibility of controversy. Good or bad, attention was what sustained her. She didn't eat; she lived or died by her follower count. Goaded by a crowd of virtual witnesses, R1nku provoked. She courted the ire of the hijras as partygoers took to watching and commenting on their holophones. Non-subscribers crowded around the edges of the action, striving for a glimpse. Bhanu shook the alms canister. A few meager coins rattled at the bottom.

"I'll tell you what's cheap. That tit job!" Iqbal and R1nku were leaning over the terrace wall, trading catty insults.

"Why don't you just make up your mind and get the cut already?" Saraswati mocked. "Cut above," she gestured to her long braid, "Or down below?" She pointed to her groin. Iqbal admired hijras, liked them even, but hijras didn't always like them: a femme boy who favored women's apparel but wasn't looking to become a girl. One time when they were walking in a sari, a gang on the street had grabbed them and threatened to cut their hair. Lobbing taunts from the second-floor terrace, they felt bold.

"It's a fine show!" Saraswati cried. "For a fair price. Donations bring blessings."

Rohan lurched up from his seated position, irate. He began to shoo the partygoers away from the periphery of the scene. Manisha, the consummate hostess, quickly stepped in and began leading guests into the main dining room. "Dessert!" she barked cheerfully.

Rohan was at the terrace wall now. In his hand, he held a small rock from the border of the grassy lawn.

Saraswati caught his gaze. "What have we here? The man who can't satisfy his wife!" Bhanu and Asma cackled obligingly. The scattering partygoers let out a collective "Ooh!" as they scurried out of the strike zone.

Rohan, speechless, let the rock fly. It narrowly missed striking Bhanu in the center of her forehead, glancing off her temple as she turned to avoid the blow.

Saraswati drew herself to her full, formidable height. Her face was flushed with rage. Muttering, she drew her thumb to her mouth and struck her nail against her front teeth. Then she spat on the ground before the colony wall. The three women turned on their heels and continued walking south down the Marg.

Manisha caught Iqbal, R1nku, and their entourage at the top of the stairs. "Can I interest you in some jalebis and chai?" she implored.

R1nku was cold. "I don't eat," she replied testily. Her handlers whisked the virtual icon out the door.

"Your event has been sufficiently enhanced by R1nku's presence. Good evening!" they chirped.

Iqbal followed out the door, sheepishly accepting a jalebi which they gobbled as they tottered after the crew. "Lovely party, dearest. Kiss!"

//////

Something in the house felt different after that night. It started with a haze, thick and misty, that gathered over the water in the stepwell. It wouldn't clear even when the vents were opened for the whole day. The air took on a smell, like copper in a rainstorm. Then came the music, a tune that neither Manisha nor Rohan recognized. The sound was tinny and old-fashioned, seeming to come from somewhere far away — but it would pipe up at odd hours of the night, when even the Aurobindo Marg was mostly quiet.

तन तान ले, मुस्कान ले, कहे सनन-नन-ननन हवा
बस ठान ले, तू जान ले, कहे सनन-नन-ननन हवा

By the end of a nervous, sleep-deprived week, Manisha thought she had heard the sound in every room of the house at different times. Rohan rebooted the wireless net three times to clear any bad signal from the audio channels in the whole-house multimedia system. He ran countless diagnostics on the ARORA system, even calling an electrician to install some bigger resistors on the circuits that powered the built-in speakers. That would suppress any line noise or interference from radio frequency signals that emanated from everyone's holophones, cash fobs, even Nitin's new canine implants.

तन तान ले, मुस्कान ले, कहे सनन-नन-ननन हवा

बस ठान ले, तू जान ले, कहे सनन-नन-ननन हवा

The music persisted, growing louder and more abruptly stopping and starting. The lights in each room began to pulse on and off erratically. The strobing effect was nauseating.

Nitin asked to sleep in Kiran's room. Manisha and Rohan tried sleeping in the study. Only Shruti seemed undisturbed. Manisha thought to ask her if she'd heard the music too, but then thought she'd best not alarm the girl. No need to invite superstition.

तन तान ले, मुस्कान ले, कहे सनन-नन-ननन हवा
बस ठान ले, तू जान ले, कहे सनन-नन-ननन हवा

Manisha did inquire with Shruti about the patio doors being left open at all hours of day and night. Shruti swore she had locked them tight but here they were, open again. Rohan put a piece of wood in the door handles so that the doors could not be pried open. The sound of rattling wood was deafening as the house fought against this restraint.

तन तान ले, मुस्कान ले, कहे सनन-नन-ननन हवा
बस ठान ले, तू जान ले, कहे सनन-नन-ननन हवा

The windows in the study seemed to buckle and flex, making the room vibrate all night long. Manisha and Rohan moved back into the master bedroom, but not for long. Auntie was becoming unpredictable. Systems mysteriously failed. Getting up to take a shit at 3 am, Rohan burned the soles of his feet so badly on the radiant flooring that he couldn't walk for three days. Manisha, startled awake by his cries of pain, stepped onto a freezing slab, the floor so cold her feet were numb by the time she reached him. The children watched slack-jawed from the mezzanine as the water in the stepwell boiled furiously and then swiftly flash-froze.

They took to wearing chappals inside the house — clean ones of course, designated for indoor use.

तन तान ले, मुस्कान ले, कहे सनन-नन-ननन हवा
बस ठान ले, तू जान ले, कहे सनन-नन-ननन हवा

The animals were increasingly agitated by the changes to the atmosphere of the house. Laddoo the dog became aggressive and bit Shruti on the hand. Obelix worried his feathers so severely he created a bald spot on his upper chest. He now shouted obscenities incessantly, agitating Kiran so much he moved the bird cage outside to the terrace. Asterix was refusing to eat her seeds and berries. She looked listless and pale, and neither sang nor spoke.

तन तान ले, मुस्कान ले, कहे सनन-नन-ननन हवा
बस ठान ले, तू जान ले, कहे सनन-नन-ननन हवा

Shruti quietly cleaned up the molting feathers and scattered feed, talking softly to the birds. Even the dog bite failed to rile her. She seemed more concerned about the idea that Laddoo might face consequences than she was about her own bleeding finger.

//////

In the following days, activity increased around the home on the opposite corner. The students who had been living there in low-rent, dilapidated apartments had been arrested last summer for disturbing the peace after a popular uprising against the new quarantine-related mobility restrictions. According to the papers, they were still in prison, though the restrictions had since been lifted. Construction quickly began on the vacant property. This meant camps of migrant men living onsite without water or plumbing until the rough demolition and reframing work was complete. After months living onsite, these people now quickly moved aside to make room for the "clean crew" of IIT grads who installed fiberoptics and copper.

Manisha and Rohan lamented the squalid conditions of the labor camp, but they were hardly relieved of their complaints when the finishing work began, and the new owners of the home began to make their presence known. The house had been purchased by a prominent gangster from Bhalswa, the massive government-created mega-slum in the north Delhi suburbs. After the fashion of French authorities in the mid-nineteenth century, modern Indian leaders in the early decades of the twenty-first century had undertaken a comprehensive relocation of the city's poor. This meant relocating them from their ancient neighborhoods and support networks and warehousing them in enormous housing complexes that were already deteriorating on the day that they opened. The result was that the city's gangs metastasized within the open-air prison, becoming more organized and more deadly than ever before.

Ganesha was a third-generation kingpin who had controlled city blocks before he was twelve years old. Now in pursuit of respectability, he had taken up residence with an entourage of virtual reality camgirls and bodyguards. Rohan was sure they were making C4, a popular synthetic street drug in the cathinone family, on the home's lower level. The same balance of centrality and seclusion that the couple craved in their choice of location now made the neighborhood a perfect base of operations for organized, illicit activity. For the most part, the gang left the neighbors alone, although their parties lasted until the late hours.

Manisha was weary of battling the hostile architecture and didn't want to initiate a new confrontation with the gang across the street. Their own house had gone momentarily quiet, and she was keen to maintain the peace. Rohan was defiant. He felt his territory encroached. He took to walking the block with the lathi in his hand as if to assert his original right to the city itself.

Late one evening, Rohan caught Shruti passing a plate of food through the gate to Raj, one of Ganesha's drivers. Already tipsy, Rohan became cross and attacked the young couple with the lathi. The plate fell to the ground. Raj scurried off into the darkness.

Afterwards, Shruti was contrite. She confessed to a feeling of sympathy for the young thug, who would stand for hours in front of his employer's vintage Bentley in the street. She had watched him buffing the car's already perfect exterior as she prepared the family's lavish meals. He was always at the ready for a mission that never seemed to come. She noticed how he never sat, relieved himself, or ate while on shift. She saw too how he would check his stringy hair and pick his teeth in the car's side view mirrors, vigilant against the slightest blemish to his person or his charge.

Shruti appreciated a man who took pride in his work. There wasn't any harm in a little neighborly outreach. Rohan, snarling, threatened to take her back to her parents' house on the spot.

Shruti was frightened. Rohan was already unsteady and seemed unpredictable. Though self-driving, the family car had a manual override and no breathalyzer lock for backup, like the newer models. He could do anything with her in the car, and no one would care. Shruti said a quiet mantra under her breath. Auntie began to cluck.

As if in response to her prayer, the house began to tremble. Not the jerk-and-slide motion of an earthquake, but a deep internal tremor emanating from the earth, all the way through the structure. The pulsing jogged the cabinets open, and objects began to slip. All the sprinklers in the main room suddenly came on in a blast of brackish water, soaking Manisha's top-of-the-line raw silk sofa. Auntie's clucking intensified. They heard the music again, tinny but loud enough to be audible over the rush of water.

तन तान ले, मुस्कान ले, कहे सनन-नन-ननन हवा
बस ठान ले, तू जान ले, कहे सनन-नन-ननन हवा

The children raced downstairs, screaming. The hysterical dog added to the commotion. Rohan felt a tingling sensation in his jaw. A thin trickle of blood tracked across his chin. He reached a finger back toward the back of his cheek and felt a chunk of flesh and loose, fragmented tooth. As he pressed, the soft scent of decay filled his nostrils.

Blanching, Rohan stuffed a tea towel into his cheek and barked at the children to put on clothes. Manisha started to hastily pack an overnight bag. Rohan grabbed the holophone and commanded Auntie to book a room for four at the Ambassador Hotel. Yes, she confirmed, pets were permitted.

The family drove hastily into the night, leaving Shruti alone in the heaving, shuddering house with a pair of traumatized, wailing parakeets. After the shaking stopped, the birds continued to shriek until well after dawn.

तन तान ले, मुस्कान ले, कहे सनन-नन-ननन हवा
बस ठान ले, तू जान ले, कहे सनन-नन-ननन हवा

Later in the day, Raj came around to check up on Shruti and apologize. His manner was gentle and contrite until he saw her shattered state. Convinced that she had been beaten, Raj demanded to inspect the house. He charged through the front door, chest puffed, ready to settle a score with the drunken egghead who had assaulted him the prior evening.

Entering the sodden ground level, his rage turned to bewilderment. Shruti, perched on the edge of the stained silk couch, burst into tears. She described her lonely night of fright as he gingerly held her hand. Raj was indignant. "They just left you here in this evil place!"

Shruti, consoled, was more sanguine. "It doesn't feel dangerous to me," she confided. "Just sad." Though young, they had both lived long enough to know sadness.

Raj stayed much of the day, cleaning up. In the evening, he was reluctant to leave Shruti in the house alone. She locked herself modestly in the tiny back bedroom.

He set himself up in the front room, lathi at the ready, primed to confront the homeowners at whatever point they might return.

तन तान ले, मुस्कान ले, कहे सनन-नन-ननन हवा
बस ठान ले, तू जान ले, कहे सनन-नन-ननन हवा

//////

Ensconced poolside at the Ambassador, Manisha pulled out her holophone. "I'll set you up with my top vastu people, not those jokers the developers use," ARORA admonished her in a clipped digital voice. "But first you need to cleanse all that negative energy. Leave it to Auntie." Manisha was relieved. She had assumed the ARORA system was faulty when they exited the house. Less than an hour later, ARORA had downloaded seventeen personalized meditation and astrology apps and the family was booked into a three-day retreat at a rural Himalayan meditation ashram in the foothills of Rishikesh.

The family disgorged from the high-speed rail car at Yog Nagari station in Rishikesh where they were met by an emissary from the Ganga Dham with a waiting electric tuk-tuk. The emissary spoke English with a vaguely European accent, and presented as indeterminate in age, ethnicity, and gender.

Dressed from head to toe in loose-fitting clothing made of saffron-colored khadi cloth, they introduced themselves as Shakti. "Greetings on behalf of the Bhagwan," they intoned.

Swiftly, five humans and a little dog were crammed into the tiny vehicle, piled high with the ramshackle stack of bags with which they had made their late-night escape. Shakti punched a set of coordinates into the autopilot and the tuk-tuk set off. It wobbled slightly on the sharp turns.

The ride took less than half an hour. The route meandered along the bank of the holy Ganges. The water was clear as they crossed over tributaries and inlets, teal soaking into grey quite unlike the sludgy brown that Manisha recalled from her youth. Serene green hills and sparkling riverbends gave way to a tourist hub where adventure sports rentals and American veggie burgers could be readily obtained. Nitin was excited to go on safari. Kiran perked up when he saw a group of bubbly European girls lingering in front of a hostel. Just as quickly, the tuk-tuk passed out of the little town and back into mountainous crevices. The two boys groaned and rolled their eyes.

Finally, they pulled up alongside a large compound nestled between the riverside and the base of a lush green mountain. Everything was white, from the stones that paved the large approach to the walls, railings, and stairs that led down to the riverbank below. Shakti stopped the tuk-tuk at the foot of one of the staircases. They were met by two more assistants in yellow, who waved ultrasonic well-being scanners in their direction. Wordlessly, the assistants reached for two of the teetering bags atop. Rohan shouldered another, Kiran a fourth, and the five of them made their way slowly up the rickety steps.

The first stop was the children's quarters at the outer perimeter of the compound. "Bhagwan prefers to keep children out of the complex entirely," Shakti admitted. "But we were able to make this private room available because it can be accessed without entering the main grounds." Their eyes sharpened as they turned toward the children. "Roam the village all you want. You'll find solar-powered electrocycles in the yard behind the hut. Come back before sundown, and don't go in the water or you might get eaten by gharials."

Kiran chuckled nervously. "Was that a joke?" he asked weakly. "I thought gharials were extinct." Shakti's silent glare affirmed that it was not. A quick holophone search confirmed that synthetically hatched crocodiles had in fact been repopulated into the river some two years prior.

Manisha and Rohan's room was similarly appointed to the children's, but Shakti informed them that its placement on the highest terrace level overlooking the river valley was evidence of their high status among the penitents currently booked into the Ganga Dham. As dusk fell, they settled into the sparsely attired double bed and pulled the mosquito netting down over the open patio door.

//////

तन तान ले, मुस्कान ले, कहे सनन-नन-ननन हवा
बस ठान ले, तू जान ले, कहे सनन-नन-ननन हवा

Raj awoke with a start and sat upright in his chair. Rattled by his own uncharacteristic somnolence, he stood, straightened his jacket, rolled a beedi, and stepped onto the veranda. The action at Ganesha's was unwaning, with the usual pack of high rollers and escorts coming and going. Pimps and prostitutes, Raj thought to himself. Then an old nemesis, Harish, caught his eye.

Harish was flashy and boisterous, a compulsive womanizer, and he idolized Ganesha, emulating the gangster's style and even his mannerisms like a living bootleg copy. Raj considered himself above this type, as a man who had earned the gangster's respect through a code of honor, not his tolerance through flattery. Tonight, from a distance, as Harish and his entourage of virtual call girls whirled out the door, Raj suddenly understood how Ganesha was more than tolerant of the younger man, how his empire was restructuring to make space for this new heir, how connectedness and amiability would inevitably win over honor, how the act of dominating or deceiving a woman was rewarded by a society of men. Raj, a social nobody, would never command that kind of power, but he could show Ganesha what kind of power he did have to wield.

He finished his smoke and went back inside, incensed.

Shortly before dawn, Shruti was awakened from sleep by an urgent rapping at her bedroom door. Assuming that the family had returned, she dressed hastily and opened the door. Instead, she found Raj, sweating and out of breath. The ARORA system clucked softly, but audibly, in the distance.

तन तान ले, मुस्कान ले, कहे सनन-नन-ननन हवा
बस ठान ले, तू जान ले, कहे सनन-नन-ननन हवा

"Dirty woman!" he rasped. "Inviting me to stay alone with you." He pushed past her slim figure in the narrow doorway, forcing his way into the tiny bedroom. Shruti was terrified. She tried not to show it. Raj's taunts stunned her. She had been swayed by his dapper appearance, his sense of duty, his kind eyes. The man before her now had none of that.

Shruti's social station often left her vulnerable to the baser impulses of men. Should she be assaulted, she expected no assistance from police, neighbors, or her employer. For this reason, she took pains to protect her modesty in every interaction. Now she was thinking on her feet.

"You look hungry, ji. The night has not been kind. You've been so helpful to me," Shruti entreated, making her voice as submissive as possible. Quickly she slipped past him and out of the bedroom, smiling lightly as she donned an apron and began to rustle through the fridge. "Please, I'm just a servant. Accept this humble offering of thanks." Shruti was careful to keep her eyes on her work, never looking at Raj directly. She worked quickly and the small space soon filled with the sting of chopped onions. Raj, coughing, backed out of the narrow kitchen space into the large front room. The clucking sound slowed, and quieted.

तन तान ले, मुस्कान ले, कहे सनन-नन-ननन हवा
बस ठान ले, तू जान ले, कहे सनन-नन-ननन हवा

Shruti served up a hot omelet and a steaming cup of chai. Raj was placated, she thought, so she left him at the table and went upstairs to prepare the bedrooms for the family's impending return.

Raj sat impatiently on the soiled silk sofa. He was a proud man. He had to live up to certain expectations that the people around him had for a man. Expectations that he should take whatever he needed, without hesitation or remorse. These burdens had never sat well with the driver, who was a quiet man by nature. But now he felt robust, ready to lift mountains.

Raj's ears perked as he heard the soft sound of singing coming from the upstairs bedroom. It grew louder as he ascended. Softly, he came up behind Shruti as she worked. He stood so close that she couldn't back up without bumping his chest. The music stopped.

"You'll be working for me now," Raj hissed. He grabbed Shruti by the arm. Twice her weight, he would easily overpower her. Fighting back would be futile. His hands were like stone against her tender skin. His fingers pressed her bone so hard she thought it would break.

As she went limp, Shruti heard the master bathroom toilet call her name. All six shower nozzles came blasting on at once. A great rumbling came from the depths of the ancient stepwell as the water began to boil.

तन तान ले, मुस्कान ले, कहे सनन-नन-ननन हवा
बस ठान ले, तू जान ले, कहे सनन-नन-ननन हवा

//////

In the morning, Shakti came to fetch Rohan and Manisha for the day's activities. They brought them each a set of loose-fitting garments in light orange khadi cloth. Everyone at the ashram was asked to wear the same garb. "It removes focus from our differences and shifts attention to our similarities," Shakti explained.

Rohan snarled at the attendant's back as they left. He didn't want to wear the costume. Manisha cajoled him. What a relief not to have to find a laundromat out here in the middle of nowhere, she pleaded. Rohan was petulant. "I'm not keen to wash your chaddis in the river like some village girl," she snapped, surprising them both. The holophone clucked beside the bed.

The morning session started out in a large open room that was bare except for tatami mats on the floor and a lotus-shaped dais at the center. Swiftly, attendants placed yoga mats throughout the space. A bell chimed and dozens of penitents appeared to take their places on their mats. Rohan and Manisha followed suit. As the attendants filtered out, one stopped to maneuver an electronic panel close to the main door. A massive hologram of Bhagwan, dressed in orange and fit as he never was in his prime, appeared on the dais. Bhagwan led the disciples in a vigorous routine of sun salutations. This was followed by deep chakra meditation, accompanied by his signature wisdom.

"Love should be like breathing," Hologram Bhagwan intoned. He drew a deep breath, a touch that Rohan found affected coming from a two-dimensional hologram. "It is not a question of being in love with someone — it is a question of being love." Manisha was struck. All her life she had focused her affections on others, first her father, then her husband, now her sons. "Even if you are alone, love goes on overflowing from you," Bhagwan continued. Manisha tried to parse what "being love" meant. She was still thinking about it when the session ended, but the hologram flickered off without taking any questions.

A set of large sliding doors made from transparent laminate opened out from the hall onto a fragrant pool, churning like an oversized hot tub. The pool was filled with naked, glistening bodies. Shakti shed their vestments, revealing their slim, androgynous frame. Manisha and Rohan did the same. The three of them stepped into the steaming water, Shakti placing floral blooms atop the currents as they waded past. Groups of disciples gathered in pairs and clusters in the scalloped banks of bench seats that lined the large pool. Some were gossiping, others bathed one another lovingly. There were people engaged in a range of sexual configurations.

Shakti stopped at an empty bank and gestured for the couple to follow. They began to rub a thick brownish-grey paste into Manisha's toffee-colored skin. The mud was dense and full of sediment. "Charcoal, haldi, and pure sea salt," they explained as they pressed the muck insistently into her pores. There was no part of her body that their gentle prodding left fallow. The wet mud shriveled as it dried, cool and cracking, pinching the tender skin on her throat and her areolae.

Rohan was next. As Shakti slathered his body in mud, another attendant began to peel the caking earth away from Manisha's skin. This attendant was similarly androgynous, striking, with glistening skin that was so dark it was nearly purple. Introducing themselves as Krshna, they proceeded to coat Manisha's body in thick, viscous oil. It smelled like cloves and cardamom. She felt her skin heating up.

Manisha suddenly felt brave. She leaned in to Krshna and asked them quietly if they could explain Bhagwan's words to her. Krshna murmured into Manisha's ear. She laughed nervously and nodded her head.

Rohan watched from the neighboring bay with alarm as Krshna began to administer a vigorous massage to Manisha's lower torso. Immobilized by shame, he felt his penis ossifying in the earth that was stuck to his pubic hair. As Krshna swiftly and repeatedly brought his wife to climax, Rohan was struck by the recognition that the old bitch on the Aurobindo Marg had been right about his lack of ability.

As Shakti cleansed Rohan's body of mud, he felt their caresses becoming more insistent. To his relief, he felt himself responding. Here was a chance to prove his virility once and for all, with witnesses. Shakti was so giving, so willing. By the time he realized he was penetrating an android, he was too far along to stop. Anyway, Rohan thought, what difference does it make?

Abruptly, a commotion started at the entrance to the hall. A third attendant in orange robes rushed forward, bearing towels. Auntie was howling from Manisha's holophone, which the kids had borrowed earlier in the day to explore the nearby town. When Auntie had called, the boys raced up the hill to tell their parents that the villa in Hauz Khas was ablaze.

//////

The CID officers sat in the driveway waiting in a grey, armored PAV pod. They had located the ARORA system's "black box" solid state storage drive in the charred remains of the villa. There were multiple agents camped out in the driveway with electronic bays trying to extract its contents. The senior most officer, a tall dark-skinned woman with extremely straight hair, introduced herself as ACP Kondavilli. Her eyes were flinty behind the greenish tint of her smart lenses.

"The system reports that the fire started in the small bedroom behind the kitchen," Kondavilli explained, reading from a report only she could see.

Manisha was coy. "That's the ayah's room," she explained. "Shruti was alone in the house for a few days while we went out of town." Manisha looked around, startled. "Where is she?"

Rohan grimaced. Wasn't it obvious? He held his tongue out of respect for the officers, and the solemnity of the news.

"We've identified two individuals at the scene," Kondavilli reported. Her face was impassive. "Both are deceased." Manisha gasped. Kondavilli continued. "We don't yet understand what happened. Our team is working on it now." The holophone in

Manisha's purse chittered frantically. Two bright pink parakeets startled and took off from a nearby jacaranda tree.

Manisha was confused. "Surely the fire…?"

Kondavilli interrupted. "The surveillance footage shows the woman going upstairs, and the man following shortly thereafter." She paused to collect her thoughts. "There's some evidence of a struggle but we can't piece together what exactly happened. It mostly took place out of frame of the bedroom camera. About 30 minutes after that, the fire started downstairs — but the cameras don't show anyone moving in the house," she said carefully. They stood silently, Manisha sobbing with her face buried in her hands.

Kondavilli interrupted again. "There's one more thing. The coroner says the burns are consistent with the early stage of cremation. This suggests that the victims were already deceased for some time before the fire started." Manisha gasped. Rohan swore. Auntie gibbered.

//////

They put the lot up for sale in July. Cleared of rubble, it was worth more in cash on the market than insurance had paid out for the destroyed structure. They used the settlement to rent a suite at the Ashok Hotel for six months in a flat-fee arrangement.

A developer from Singapore bought the property as-is. She already owned three adjoining lots and was planning to tear down the other houses to build a new luxury mall. The historic stepwell, temporarily drained, would be a defining feature.

In their executive suite at the Ashok, Manisha updated her holophone to the latest Sonic and Holographic Responsive User Telephone Interface. SHRUTI recommended seventeen undergraduate programs for which they could successfully optimize their older child's chances of admission. Three were in China. Twelve were in the United States and Canada. Two were in Europe. In December, Kiran was accepted early decision to a small liberal arts college in western Massachusetts.

Rohan, reluctant to go back to the States, had put Shakti to work researching fellowship opportunities in Europe, but Manisha was enthused about the Northeast. People there had good breeding; wasn't that why they were called "brahmins"? In any case, she thought, the family should stay together. SHRUTI booked air passage for five plus the dog, then kissed Manisha goodnight.

PROPERTY VALUES

MONICA

On Saturdays in July, Mom and Del have been taking the LynkPod down to Sherman Oaks. They come back late, giggling and drunk, and I pretend I'm asleep, so they don't stop talking. There's something different about the adults on those nights. They don't say much about where they go — Mom says they're doing charity work but sometimes they come home smelling like alcohol. Then they get all excited, and they make a lot of noise all night long.

On Sunday, I ask Mom again what they do on Saturday night. She gets kind of quiet and then she says, "You don't need to worry about the world out there, Monica. It's peaceful up here. Don't take it for granted." Then her eyes get cold and she stands up and puts the news on the old streaming television in my bedroom. "Del is helping me," she tells me earnestly. "And we're helping people." Mom sighs with disgust. "Honestly, people are animals." I don't know if she's talking about people downtown fighting over food rations on the television, or herself, or me, but since we moved here, I feel like a house pet.

Downstairs, Sam is monopolizing the living room, rigged into the Hypersurround. He seems to always be wired in, doing who knows what. I don't know how to use much of the tech in the house. The adults are always busy, so I usually end up negotiating with him to get information or help to access the leisure system. I don't use the Hypersurround because Mom doesn't like it. She says everything in the Hyperverse costs money, which we don't have.

Later, when we're cleaning up after lunch, I ask Sam why Mom says people are animals, but his answer doesn't make a lot of sense. "The bonobo shares 98.7 percent of human DNA," he informs me. I ask him if he knows what Mom and Del get up to on Saturday nights when they leave us alone with LICI, the voice- and camera-activated home assistant.

Sam activates the voice assistant. "Bonobos use sexual contact to defuse conflicts and strengthen social bonds," LICI explains. Sam turns away and starts rearranging the assembly to plug back into the Hypersurround.

I move a little closer. Sex is something I didn't used to care about, but I want to understand what's keeping us here in this empty, creepy house that watches me 24/7.

Sam looks at me curiously. His scent makes the hair on the back of my neck stand up. Sam's about my age, and he doesn't have family here, only Del. All I've got is Mom.

It's been just us for as long as I can remember. We move a lot.

Sometimes we live by ourselves, sometimes not. Usually when we move, it happens quickly, and without warning. Someone, usually not Mom, eventually tells me what's happening long after I figure things out on my own. Sometimes it's another kid, sometimes an adult. Sometimes they want to help me, sometimes they want something that I can give them. Bartering what little I have for information is second nature by now.

When the drought got worse, and the food riots started in the city, we came up here. We've never lived in a house like this, with land. It's rural but upscale. I've never had a room this big, all to myself. It's been a couple months and I'm still not used to being here. It's cold and white and bare. I suppose it was beautiful until the landscape burned.

SAM

Before the fires, I'd roam the grounds endlessly until someone had a use for me. People came to work, tutored me, fed the animals and such. Mr. Kelly and the ranch hands were on the property almost every day. I rode my horse Callisto, played tennis, went to social functions and restaurants. Now the livestock and the orchards are dead and the whole world's come inside. No one comes to work. School went online. Everything happens through LICI, on a screen, on a holodeck, or in the rig. It's both claustrophobic and totally empty.

Once we'd been inside for a few months, Del renovated the house to provide for all our needs. Biosensors, cameras, microphones, and RFID chips are built into every inch. Since the flames died down they've been spending more time out, but I can't leave. I have nowhere to go. In the house, LICI's eyes are on me constantly when no one's around.

At least before Elizabeth and Monica moved in I had the downstairs and the Hypersurround to myself. I'm more comfortable in isolation now. When I get lost in the network, it's like I fuse with the rig. Lose the body and forget how much I miss the sense of touch. As much as I can, I spend all my time in the Hyperverse. I even sleep there, dreaming inside the dreamscape, deep beneath an ocean of packets and pixels.

In the Hyperverse, I'm never alone. Everyone's eyes are on me, but it's different. I've built everything that I touch. I own everyone that I meet. The best part is, I control how they see me. I can even change who it is that they see.

Del believes in science. That's why they had me in a lab. They told me when I was seven. Del likes to say that reproductive labor is a form of abuse. I'm not sure what they're talking about, but I found a hard drive with my DNA sequence in it in the attic, packed with some hair and skin samples from the horses that died last fall.

Del is a leader in the community. They're known for supporting causes, candidates, and people in need. Sometimes they bring home friends, like Elizabeth. Women who have fallen on hard times come to Del for their generosity and guidance. I had hoped the flow of temporary lodgers might stop when the rain did but now that the flames have burned out and the drought is long-term, they say there's a lot more need. Someone new moves in every few months. They don't usually have kids, but Del said we have space for more now that I'm not using the bedroom. They weren't going to discuss the living arrangements any further.

They still haven't asked me why I stopped sleeping in the bedroom.

Del always tells people they're raising a different kind of man. I'm not like every other boy. I was born with two X chromosomes and a Y. Del doesn't believe in gender, but they said they would pay for medical treatment to affirm a gender "if you make a decision." I'm not "deciding." I'm not a girl. Girls are soft and anxious, looking for a place in the world. I'm a boy.

In the Hyperverse, where anyone can inhabit any gender, the differences between men and women become even more clear. There are two kinds of people — subjects and objects. It's not about biology. Either you act or you're acted upon.

Of course, I took the scrip from the doctor's office. Androgens can be a rush. But I use it sparingly. I don't want to get too used to one reality. I want to keep control of my own body. Del and LICI control everything else about my life.

Men on the street used to notice how I'm different. They would make their interest known. I guess that's the upside of testosterone. I didn't mind that they liked me. They didn't know me, and Del didn't know about them. It was good as long as I could keep control. But that didn't always happen; there's a lot of risk outside. After the world moved inside, I thought I'd be more protected from men's eyes and their unpredictable intentions.

Girls are different though, they don't make themselves clear. I haven't offered Monica anything, and I'm not sure what she's after.

I've never had a girl look at me like she saw something she would want before. But there's no way a girl like that knows anything about the world I live in. No one does, not even Del. That's why the Hyperverse is a safe place for me.

MONICA

Since we moved in, I've been sleeping in Sam's room. He sleeps on the couch downstairs. Mom and I were supposed to share the room, but after a couple of weeks she started sleeping in the master suite with Del. Sam said he wasn't using the bedroom. He has a lot of expensive things he doesn't seem to use.

The room is cold at night. Sometimes when I can't sleep, I put on this red t-shirt I found in his drawer and wear it to bed. I've never seen Sam wear it, but it still smells like him. I always fold it up and put it back in the morning, all the way at the bottom. I've had a lot of sleepless nights this week.

When I get home from my Saturday afternoon shift at the call center, Sam is wearing my sleep shirt. I cringe, but then I bluff. I knew he'd find me out eventually.

His golden eyes are soft as they follow me around the living room. I feel like I'm going to throw up. I haven't spent a lot of time around men in my life. In the city, the men we met whether young or old were usually in a gang or a militia, all fear wrapped in cruelty, and best to avoid.

I don't know what to expect from Sam, who spends all his time in this strange empty house, wired into some other place that no one else can see. I make myself unapproachable while I try to figure this out.

"Have you ever been online?" he asks me quietly, which is more than Sam usually says to me in a week, unless I ask a question that leads to some weird fact. I brush him off and go to the kitchen to get a smoothie from the subscription tap. We get drinks on demand up here. Our last place didn't have drinkable water.

When I come back, Sam asks again. I shake my head. He looks disappointed. He gestures me over to where he's laid out the plug-in hardware.

"This part is the sensory immersion chamber," he explains. "These triggers help you navigate." The setup is covered with a fine, silvery net, stretched between hard rubber conduits. I point to it.

"That's the haptic stimulation mesh," Sam explains. "It tells your body how things feel, when they're happening."

I run the strange fabric between my fingers. It feels delicate and brittle, like nylon run through with steel wool. After a beat, I start to get the full meaning of what he's telling me.

"So — people have sex in the Hyperverse?" I ask.

"Constantly." Sam shrugs.

"Why?" I wonder why people still want to touch in Hyperspace, where everything is virtual and ephemeral.

Sam sees my discomfort. "To defuse conflicts and strengthen social bonds." He takes the mesh bodysuit out of my hands. The Hyperverse sounds more like the real world than I was anticipating.

Sam's messing with me now. "Did you know that conservatives have more sex than liberals?" Our little mountain town prides itself on being a red spot amid the Southern California blue. Everyone up here seems so secure and comfortable, while the city tears itself apart.

I miss Los Angeles. I want to go home. I want to break something. I look Sam in the eye and ask him what happens if someone kills you in the Hypersurround.

"You die," he says simply. I'm intrigued.

"What's that like?" I ask. I spent a lot of time wanting to die when I was in middle school, but I always got scared and I could never go through with it. I still think about what it would feel like, to just stop being, stop hurting.

Sam turns away, stiffening at my visible interest. "I can't explain that. You'll have to find out yourself." The late afternoon sunlight drenches us both in its lazy heat.

I have so many questions. But I don't want to ask them when Mom and Del are around. Upstairs, the adults can hear everything we do and say.

SAM

On the last Saturday in July, the LynkPod is late. Del and Elizabeth are arguing as they scurry out the door. Irritation hangs in the air like gunpowder for another ten minutes after they leave.

Monica's on the couch, in my space. She looks uptight. She pulls a curl off her face and tucks it behind her ear. It's cute. I like her doe eyes and bad attitude. I know I started trouble by showing her the rig. I thought it would make her stop asking me questions, but then she got interested. Now she wants to try the Hypersurround, but Elizabeth isn't having it. She and I have been waiting for a night when we know they'll be gone for a while.

Now that they're gone, a beer from the subscription tap will help chill things out. Del has the tap fingerprint-locked, but given the closeness of our DNA profiles, LICI doesn't always tell our prints apart. I manage to get a pint and a half of IPA before it locks me out.

MONICA

Sam hands me a beer. It's IPA, which I hate, but I hold my breath and drink it quickly. The beer leaves a bitter aftertaste. I try not to make a sour face and fail.

Sam sits down next to me on the sofa and turns on the Hypersurround. "Where do you want to go first? We need to set you up with an avatar, then buy you some clothes and gear." I step into the rubber suit, and Sam puts the sensory immersion chamber over my eyes and ears. A vast, tiled white space appears all around me, a shopping mall but bigger, the size of a whole town. There are whole wings dedicated to shoes, wigs, clothes, and appearance. I turn toward the appearance section and see a row of glass cases containing perfectly coiffed heads in an array of styles, each with a full and intricate beat applied to his or her face.

After a moment, I feel a vibration just above my left collarbone. I turn and see a tall, stylishly dressed woman with olive skin and long black hair, tapping me on the shoulder. She chooses a face from among those displayed, detaching her own and swapping it for another with the touch of a finger.

Sam, in the guise of this avatar, grabs my arm and leads me toward a brightly lit gallery of shops. "A lot of what you can buy for women is either really high-end, or kind of messed up. Like, not very practical," he says. I ask him what he means. I really wish I knew anything about this world. Why is Mom so against the Hypersurround? Sam seems to know so much more about everything than I do.

"Let's see," I venture. I'm not feeling very confident, but I want to look cool. I choose a lace corset, jeans, and boots for my avatar, with brown skin, white makeup, and orange hair. I want the long, white alpaca coat in the shop window, but it's out of my price range. In the accessories row, I nab a pair of silvery butterfly wings.

SAM

In the Hyperverse, everything feels real, but better. Even dying.

The first time I died was after Mr. Kelly put my horse down. The drought had evaporated the creek that runs through the ranch. The remaining sludge had become infested with fungus, and the horses had all developed thrush.

Del took me to help Mr. Kelly with Callisto. They said they wanted me to understand the responsibility that we wield, as a species, and as a family. Del held me firm while Mr. Kelly drove the pneumatic hammer into her forehead, right between her sweet brown eyes. I knew enough not to cry in front of them.

A couple days later, Mr. Kelly found me in the barn. I was crying — I was forgetting to keep it inside. He said I was weak, a liability to Del. He promised to toughen me up.

I left my body when he touched me, and I almost didn't come back. I'm more careful about feeling my emotions now. You never know who's watching when you think you're alone.

There are some things in Hyperspace that I don't think Monica will like, but if she asks me, I have to show her. I can't tell her what her limits are. That would be patronizing. I try to come up with some language. Dr. Chakrovarty, LICI's behavioral therapy language bot, has a conflict code: "green light, yellow light, red light." I used to hear Del and their friends say "red light" sometimes after a particularly loud date, that was before I started sleeping in the Hypersurround. I can't hear anything Del says or does from inside the rig.

"If you want to stop, say 'red light' okay? We don't have to do anything you don't want to do," I tell her, gently.

Monica exhales sharply. "Okay." She's holding onto my hand pretty tightly. I think about how to help her relax.

I take the beer glasses back to the kitchen. This time the subscription tap fills them both all the way. As I pass the refrigerator, I pop a T-jelly from the cabinet. The lid of the bottle scans my thumbprint before opening. Testosterone tastes like strawberries and iron on my tongue.

Monica likes the rig. Like me, she's excited by the possibilities that it offers for reinventing herself into someone stronger and more authoritative. But building your ideal persona is expensive. The Hyperverse is fueled by currency and there are different ways to get it. You can buy it with hard coin, you can steal it, or you can earn it.

I've given Monica the basics as a courtesy — an avatar, some basic customization, and a few hyperbux in her pocket. But I can't float her forever, and I wouldn't recommend she make her money the way that I do. Not everyone has the stomach for the violent and profitable world of Gladia.

Our first stop is the galleria zone, which all hyperspaces require as an entry point into their reality. This is where you customize and build your avatar for each session. Creators can build as many realities as they can design. Some have puzzles and challenges to win, others are more transactional, but generally all hyperspaces are structured around the dopamine loop of earning and spending hyperbux. The more you win, the more you want.

I don't want visitors to my Hyperspace to know about Monica. If they know we're associated outside the Hyperverse, it could be dangerous for her. That's why I've chosen to incarnate as a woman today. As the t-spike starts to crest, I consider changing back to my normal, masculine shape, but I also don't want Monica to know that I own this Hyperspace. She could weaken and tell Elizabeth what she saw, and I don't want it getting back to Del that I created any of this.

I own several thousand acres in the Hyperverse. Del bought me a parcel as a birthday gift when the system first shipped, and after a few months I was able to buy the land on all sides of it. After I put in some shops, nightclubs, a sports arena, and an art gallery, the value of my property started to accelerate, and it became more competitive to secure the parcels all around it. By then, I was living fully in the Hyperverse, and I wasn't about to let some corporate bots crowd my space. I needed to increase my capital flow quickly. That's when I built the Coliseum.

Monica's not into sports. We dance for a while at one of the clubs, which is fun, except people keep hitting on us and trying to offer us drug patches. I don't buy hyperdrugs on the street. Popular right now is hypercrank, which is cut with neurostimulants that burn your neurons out. People take that stuff while rigged up and stroke out, and by the time anyone on the outside figures out what's happening, they've flatlined. When hyperdrugs kill you, you don't wake up. I open a chat window and notify my security team while Monica is watching the 4D demo render competition on the main stage.

"Let's get out of here," Monica tugs at my elbow. We exit the dark nightclub into the perennial Hyperverse twilight. I'm leading her toward the art gallery and other downtown sights when she spots the Coliseum on the outer ring of the hyperspace, at the foot of the mountains. "What's that?" she asks. The theater is about to open, after which a boisterous procession will lead the evening's conscripts to the arena.

To answer her, I have to show her. Gladia is what the Hyperverse is all about. The arena is massive, with thousands of spectators cheering on their favorite fighters. Each battle is broadcast live throughout the Hyperverse, seen by millions of players.

As in Roman times, the gladiators are usually players who have broken the law. They violated the terms of the Hyperverse by running up debts, peddling hypercrank, or physically assaulting other visitors. As a Hyperverse administrator, I could simply banish them, but it's both more entertaining and more lucrative to make a ritual out of digital slaughter. Tonight's conscripts are a thin, green-skinned boy in harem pants and a toque, and a lavender-skinned, elf-eared girl in a tight miniskirt, a bra, and large animated earrings. They've been caught stealing hyperbux in a designer upgrade scam that left several avatars without functional haptics, forcing them to replace their whole rigs. The sentries lead the gladiators into the arena and surround them, the crowd chanting softly.

"Stop." Monica whispers urgently in my ear. I hit pause and pull off the sensory headset. My pulse is racing.

She speaks carefully. "Are they going to hurt them?" Monica is pale.

"Their avatars might die, but they can reincarnate. They're not banned for life," I explain.

"How do they kill them?" she whispers.

I shrug. "The gladiators more or less tear one another apart. It's pretty gruesome, you don't have to watch it."

"And people pay to watch this?" Monica is a quick study.

I laugh. "Some people enjoy watching other people suffer, even if the pain isn't real." I'm answering cautiously, trying not to answer what she hasn't asked me yet.

"Do you enjoy it?" She asks me pointedly.

"In a sense. I think pain you can turn off is better than pain you can't turn off." That's what makes the Hyperverse my preferred reality.

MONICA

This wasn't the answer I anticipated. What Sam was doing seemed like fun, but watching the hungry cruelty of the arena, I'm haunted. Perhaps humans are worse than animals. Animals are never cruel. For a moment I question how much more I want to see, but curiosity wins out.

"Red light?" He looks concerned. "You've had enough."

"No. I'm okay. Let's go do something else." When he turns off the Hypersurround, I don't want this to be the last image in my head. I still have questions I want answered and I can't lose my nerve.

We walk around the art gallery and Sam shows me who the famous artists are. Downtown, we browse the shops. I want to buy a necklace, but I don't have enough hyperbux, so Sam buys it for me. At the waterfront, the ocean is teal and purple, with glints reflecting the eternally grey sky. He touches my arm.

"If you think you want to stay here, you need to find a way to earn some money," he admonishes me. "You should figure out what kind of job you want to do." People work as shopkeepers, stylists, maintenance crews, and cooks in the Hyperverse, earning hyperbux that they can spend on accessories and experiences. But I'm not interested in an honest living.

"If you die in the arena, what happens to your debt?" I can't stop thinking about what we saw. I think I know the answer, but I want Sam to confirm it.

"Your debts are erased when you die. You come back with a clean slate. But you don't have any of your stuff, or any money." I can live with that. What I can't afford, I can borrow or steal. Outside, you don't get second chances this easily.

I run back toward the shops and make for the alpaca coat. I walk into the store, grab the coat off the mannequin, and walk out into the street. No one stops me or says a word. I put on my coat, spin around, and turn back toward the waterfront where Sam is waiting with a baffled expression. Out of nowhere, a swarm of security agents surrounds me as I walk across the sand toward him.

"Stop! Don't touch her." Suddenly the tall, elegant woman disappears, and a strapping, suited man appears in her place. He's twice my size, blond, with biceps the size of trash cans. His suit, clearly expensive, is holoprinted with interlocking "G"s. At the sight of him, the security agents scatter. The lead agent, whose coat is red instead of black, stammers deferentially as he recedes into the horizon. Whatever Sam's role is in the Hyperverse, these cops are afraid of him.

"You don't need to act out, Monica," Sam admonishes me. "You can go anywhere in the Hyperverse, you just need to ask." He waves his hand and we're inside the Coliseum.

Attendants dressed in gold and ivory surround me. They strip me of my clothes, bathe and dress me in a white, transparent sheath. Outside, I'd be self-conscious, but here I feel regal in my naked skin.

In the arena, I can feel eyes watching me, and I marvel at the way the haptic mesh electrifies my skin under the gaze of the crowd. Under the digital moonlight, the gladiators tear my body apart, piece by piece. With each excision, I feel my memory getting shorter, and my desire getting stronger. When there are no parts left to remove, I feel relief, an unspeakable lightness. Unburdened by a body, I am the current, I am the flow.

I reincarnate with a jolt. Another body, another cage but I can't free myself again until the moon rises tomorrow night. At least Sam's put some hyperbux in my wallet. I could get used to this arrangement.

It's getting late. Sam turns off the Hypersurround. When I pull off the mesh bodysuit, my skin is red and drenched with sweat. Sam flushes at the sight of my bare chest, but I don't feel shy, I feel regal.

I've never met anyone who liked dying as much as I do. He built a whole world around dying and he lives inside it. I want to die with him over and over, all day and all night.

Sam's touch brings me back into my body. Without realizing it, I'm caught up in movement, forgetting to set boundaries. His hands are fast, and everywhere. I can still see the arena in my mind's eye, can hear attendants whispering into my dismembered ears.

Fuse with us, burn the flesh. Automate. Reproduce. Proliferate.

I dream hydraulics. Fluid dynamics. Heat. Flame. Combustion. Purple, orange, white, red.

"Red light." I've left myself too open. The city, with its everyday fear and hunger, is so close. I want safety, and protection. I need some guarantees. I won't just be discarded if the situation becomes inconvenient.

A siren howls in the distance. The hillside burns afresh.

Emotion is a reaction and a strategy. There are tears. Sam holds me close and reassures me until I fall asleep.

SAM

Everyone and everything in this house belongs to Del. Only they have the power to give and take away. Their punishments never come when and where I expect.

When they come back, LICI will give them a full report of our activities, and if they're paying attention, they'll add things up. I have learned to distract them with small misbehaviors, so they get all worked up and overlook the bigger transgressions. But Del isn't where my attention is right now. The dim awareness that nothing happens without them eventually finding out is obscured by my intense curiosity about every inch of this girl.

Monica sleeps, and my anger returns. Power is exquisite. In its grip love becomes more terrible and more perfect. Fusion with another body, loss of self, it doesn't last. But in the aftermath, power's exercise can resurrect that beautiful tension. To make a living person your very own object, to take their life, it's awe-inspiring.

You either act or you're acted upon. Love is a shield, and a blade.

The hormone boost makes the fury hotter and sharper. I hold Monica's actual life in my hands, not because I can be trusted with it — I can't — but because I was born with a place in the world, and she wasn't. I can't call it an accident of birth. Nothing about my birth has been an accident. Some people control everything, have all the resources, peace, and security. Others can be reduced to dust, without warning, on a whim. For the first time, I understand why the people are at war.

I'm much too careless with this power that I didn't earn, but everyone offers me. I've been refusing that burden passively, through childishness and incompetence. A man needs to be more strategic, and more subversive.

I take leave of the body that binds me to this brutal world and rise into the night sky. I see the house, the barn, the fire line, the lights of the city peeking through the smoke, the man-made flames on the southern edge. I can feel the void of space and looking back I see myself and Monica infinitesimally small inside our hilltop prison.

The LynkPod goes silently whooshing past. The body yanks the tether and I land, hard.

Del and Elizabeth are unusually subdued as they walk up the drive. I disentangle, savoring the last moment of skin on skin. With their return comes a regime of control and distance. Our next chance to be together could take time, and we will have to be patient.

The warmth of our love is chilled by the tension that Del and

Elizabeth bring into the house. They never really seem happy together. I wonder what each of them gets from the other that they need but don't ever seem to want. I think about Monica's body like an ocean, bathing in her, drowning in her.

Stumbling into the upstairs bathroom, I pretend to brush my teeth. Del says an abrupt "Hi" as they come down the hall. They look startled, as though they thought they saw their own reflection. Elizabeth won't make eye contact with me. She looks pinched as she passes me in the doorway. I offer a lifeless smile in return.

I go downstairs and pack up the extra rig, put the beer glasses in the dishwasher. I start the wash and set the coffee timer. I make my bed up on the sofa and wire myself in for the night.

Afterword

Use Me at Your Own Risk is a novel set in a near-future where both automation and climate collapse are more advanced. Bringing to life the ethical challenges inherent in our unprecedented shift to automation, I sought to explore the intersection of racial and gender-based social violence with our growing technology addiction, and the risks that unregulated pornography and dark web access pose to young people and families. The novel is set in 2046. This is the year that the United States population is projected to pass 50% nonwhite residents and the global sea level is projected to rise by up to two feet. Far from technophobic, the novel takes an accelerationist approach to compounding anxieties about environmental, political, and public health catastrophes to illustrate potential outcomes of the everyday moves we are making in favor of comfort and away from survival.

Sexuality and intimacy, interfamilial relationships, faith, affluence, and class are at the heart of every chapter, each of which takes place in a world that is mostly like our own except for a few key biotechnological differences. Individual stories describe events in disparate locations including Oakland, New Delhi, Los Angeles, Silicon Valley, and the North Atlantic. The locations and subjects are informed by my ongoing interest in globalization through digitization, embodiment as a political paradigm, and the queer family as a site of resistance to social reorganization by artificial general intelligences and widespread automation.

The novel was written during the COVID-19 quarantine in 2020-21. I chose a realist style informed by internet prose and journalistic conventions that enable me to describe speculative fiction scenarios in vivid, believable detail. In places, I am experimenting with the authorial voice in the age of automation by employing search engine optimization language, early GPT software, and appropriation, our post-internet version of the cut-up technique. The purpose of using storytelling and fiction to describe potential future outcomes is to alert people to their ability to make different choices now, communicating through emotional instead of rational cues in an age when the public is experiencing climate and pandemic fatigue.

Novelists like J.G. Ballard, Octavia Butler, Philip K. Dick, Kathy Acker, and William Gibson informed my thinking long before critical theory did, and this project marks a return to the form that launched me as a reader and a writer. As a cultural critic and professor, I have focused on critical posthumanist and feminist new materialist philosophy, proponents of which (such as Jane Bennett, Rosi Braidotti, Tiziana Terranova, Katherine McKittrick, and Helen Hester) argue that feminist, queer, and anti-racist politics should inhabit the material substance, not only the overt content of artistic and creative forms. I am equally motivated by a deep frustration at the state of current media discourses on artificial intelligence and climate collapse, which too often cultivate hysteria about unlikely-but-dramatic scenarios while ignoring real and urgent, but boring, realities in the present day. I consider this book to be an activist art project.

Having lived through multiple technological revolutions in the first half of my life, this project is prompted by the role that novels and short stories had in sparking my own youthful interest in posthuman ideas. I see parallels with myself as a teen in the undergraduate students I teach, few of whom read art writing but all of whom consume media and read and express a deep interest in understanding their world. This book can capture their imaginations and inform a different future.

The novel form appeals because one can influence the non-theoretically minded reading public through stories, and the non-reading public through future adaptation into film, television, or video games. The potential readership for a speculative fiction novel is broader and more diverse than that for even the most accessible art writing. I am especially hoping to reach Gen Z readers who will be the age I am now in 2046.

My writing is moving from nonfiction arts criticism into autofiction, creative nonfiction, and science fiction as the readership for arts writing becomes ever narrower and more rigid. This shift was accelerated during the pandemic, when surreal daily experiences, technological ubiquity, and long stretches of undifferentiated time became the norm. In that cultural space, art criticism felt ever more hermetic and limited in its imaginative and experimental potential. Fiction, by comparison, felt fresh and innovative, and allowed me to say what criticism cannot, which is how it feels to be alive right now. Only art can do that.

Anuradha Vikram is a writer, curator, and educator based in Los Angeles, CA. Vikram's book *Decolonizing Culture* (Sming Sming Books, 2017) helped initiate a global movement to decolonize arts institutions and monuments. They have written for art periodicals and publications from Paper Monument, Heyday Press, Routledge, and Oxford University Press. They are an Editorial Board member at *X-TRA*, and faculty in the UCLA School of the Arts and Architecture. They hold an MA in Curatorial Practice from California College of the Arts and a BS in Studio Art from NYU.

USE ME AT YOUR OWN RISK: visions from the darkest timeline
by Anuradha Vikram

Published in June, 2023 by X Artists' Books, Los Angeles

This publication is part of X Artists' Books' X Topics (XT) series, a collection of single-author books focused on the writing and ideas of artists of color and other marginalized voices.

Cover Illustration: Isip Xin
Design & Typesetting: Margaret Tedesco
Managing Editor: Addy Rabinovitch
Copyediting: Olivia Weber-Stenis

Printed by Bookmobile
Typeset in Trajan Pro and Minion Pro.

Book: © 2023 X Artists' Books. All rights reserved. No part of this book may be reproduced, stored in a retrieval system, or transmitted in any form or by any means, electronic, mechanical, photocopying, recording or otherwise, without prior written authorization of the publisher.

USE ME AT YOUR OWN RISK text & afterword: © 2023 Anuradha Vikram
Foreword: © 2023 Addy Rabinovitch & Alexandra Grant
Cover Illustration: © 2023 Isip Xin

Library of Congress Cataloging-in-Publication Data is available on request.

ISBN: 978-1-7378388-7-6

X Artists' Books
PO Box 3424
South Pasadena, CA 91031
USA
www.xartistsbooks.com